OTHERGIRL

OTHERGIRL

Nicole Burstein

ANDERSEN PRESS • LONDON

First published in 2015 by
Andersen Press Limited
20 Vauxhall Bridge Road
London SW1V 2SA
www.andersenpress.co.uk

2 4 6 8 10 9 7 5 3 1

British Library Cataloguing in Publication Data available.

ISBN 978 1 78344 061 0

Printed and bound in Great Britain by CPI Group (UK) Ltd,
Croydon CRO 4YY

To my parents,
credit where credit is due

I've started to do a new thing where I pretend to ignore her when she taps on my window. It's funny to sense her getting quietly furious while she's hovering out there, hair illuminated blazing gold by the garden security light, while I carry on with homework. Of course it's not all that funny for long because Erica's quiet fury quickly turns to an irritated pounding on the glass.

As if I wouldn't let her in. I sigh and roll my eyes, frustrated that she's turned up at precisely the time when I've found a groove in this English essay, then go to open the catch.

'You weren't out all that long,' I say. 'No mega-villains to vanquish this evening?'

'Yeah, right,' Erica huffs as she flies through the window before letting herself collapse in a heap on my rug. 'The mega-villains would never come to this place. The worst kind of trouble we get in this town are those kids who hang about the cemetery smoking things they shouldn't. And I'm not going over there. It's creepy.'

Sometimes I think we're just like any other pair of best friends, totally different people but similar enough to make it work. We balance each other out: me with my proficiency in all things school related, and Erica with her, well...non-proficiency. Despite our differences, we're as close as sisters. Of course there is one major difference between us, one that takes a little bit of working around and patience on my part: my best friend is a freaking superhero.

We're talking powers and everything, just like those superheroes you see on the news. For Erica, it's the ability to fly and shoot flames out of her hands, which as far as we can tell is a pretty unique power among the Vigils. The ones that we know of anyway. I like to think that my superpower is the ability to craft her outfits and manage Erica's increasingly erratic work/life balance. Erica, on the other hand, is absolutely made for all this superhero stuff. She's pretty much perfect for it, to be honest; she has the whole moral-compass thing as well as the good looks. One day she's going to join the Vigil A-team and be a huge star.

I'd be a rubbish superhero. I'd get too nervous and not know what to say, or somehow manage to do entirely the wrong thing while trying to do the right thing. Plus they'd have to get me a stool to stand on for the photo shoots and promotional posters. Or get me child-size costumes, and I really don't need any more reminders that I've probably reached my optimum height potential a few centimetres too short. But that doesn't stop me wishing every now and again that I could be super-special in my own way. I'd never take Erica's powers away from her, but I just wish sometimes – OK, lots of times – that I had something, anything, that was mine that she was jealous of. Something that made me stand out, all by myself.

I do this thing sometimes, where I try and test out if I could have powers too. I can't tell Erica about it, because she'd only tell me that having a superpower is more trouble than I can imagine, and how she wishes that she was 'normal' like me. We talk about lots of things, but we never talk about what it might be like if I could fly too, or if I could see and do things that even she couldn't.

Once I tried to walk through my bedroom wall. I know it sounds absolutely ridiculous, but at the time it made sense. In science we were learning about atomic structure, and how the space between atoms is actually just vast emptiness. So if I'm mostly just empty space, and that wall over there is mostly just empty space too, then why on earth can't I walk through it? Needless to say I tried it once and then never again (it takes a surprising amount of concentration just to stop yourself bracing your arms out in front of you). I ended up with a painfully squished nose and a bit of a bruised ego too.

There was also the playing-card thing. This one I'm ashamed to say has been tried more than once. I sit with the cards laid out in front of me face down on my rug, and

I stare at them as hard as I can. But of course nothing happens. The cards don't levitate. They don't spontaneously combust. And they certainly don't psychically imprint their hidden faces on my mind, which is the power I most hope for. Just a glimmer of *something* would be nice. A flicker of spades, a hint of hearts. Anything to indicate that I'm one of the chosen ones, destined to be an almighty Vigil. But every time the cards just sit there, flat and unmoving.

'So anyway,' Erica starts as I delve into my laundry bin to retrieve the bag of her clothes that I keep hidden under my own dirty ones, 'I went to the tunnel to practise some moves, and apparently I still can't do the flame-throwing thing upside down without burning my elbows. Which reminds me, are you up for some patching?'

Erica lifts up her arms to reveal holes with singed edges in the black Lycra of her outfit. I give her the *Not again* look. She shrugs her shoulders as if to say, *What? I can't help it*, in return. I inspect the charred remnants of her sleeves. Unsurprisingly there's not a welt on the skin underneath. Erica is almost impervious to burning. We still haven't quite worked out the limit of her flame retardancy yet. I often wonder what she's really capable of, but then I shudder because I really don't want to think of a time when she'd ever need to go that far.

'I can probably get the suit patched up by the end of the weekend,' I offer, thinking about that history essay that

4

needs doing, and the maths homework too.

Of course I have to do everything twice, because Erica doesn't have an awful lot of time to get all her work done herself. After an evening like this, she'll copy whatever I've written out in her own handwriting, all tailored to give her a perfect B grade, or sit at the computer and paraphrase one of my essays so that it's suitably Erica-like to hand in without raising any suspicions.

'What about Friday? Then I can go out on Saturday night for a bit of a fly-around,' Erica suggests.

'But we've got that essay due on Friday, remember? I'm not sure I can manage it all before then.'

'OK, fine. Saturday night then? And have you thought about adding that pocket for my mobile too? Did we find out if Velcro would work?'

'Velcro's flammable unfortunately.'

'Damn it. Velcro would have been good. I guess it will have to be a zip pocket then.'

'Yup. But seriously, are you really going to be answering your phone while you're up in the air?'

'What if Jay calls?' Erica catches my raised eyebrow. 'OK, so what if you need to call me while I'm up and about? You know, to tell me where the trouble is?'

I admit she has a point, even if I do disapprove of her mentioning her latest crazy boy crush while she's in Super Mode. Seriously, that girl can't go more than five minutes without thinking about Jay. He's not even in our year. He's in the sixth form, and Erica and her friends follow him around like ducklings after a mother duck. I'd never be caught dead mooning like that over a boy.

Erica gets changed into her civilian clothes and, as is routine, she turns round and lets me undo the zip at the back of her outfit. It's an old Halloween costume and originally came with a tail and kitten-ear headband, but I've been customising the hell out of it over the last few months. I replaced the original flimsy zip with one that was sturdier and, obviously, we chucked the tail away. We adapted the collar so that it came up higher around the neck, and I even managed to sew in a rudimentary sports bra, which frankly was a bit of a textile engineering miracle on my part. I'd endured an entire evening of Erica moaning at me about what a pain flying unsupported was, and how she was sick of thinking about what was going on 'up there' when she was airborne. We looked online at the galleries of the mega-babe Vigils like the Red Rose and Hayley Divine, and honestly we don't understand how they manage to look so super-perky and comfortable while wearing so little. Must be a super-technology Vigil thing my amateur sewing skills aren't up to.

Every week, when both my parents are out, I go into the garden and spray the black catsuit down with a flame-retardant chemical spray I found at the DIY depot. Once I accidentally sprayed my dad's prize perennials and they all died overnight, so I had to invent some story about toxic fox poo so that he wouldn't investigate. After all the hard work I've already put into that costume, Erica's still nagging me about accessory pockets for her phone and keys and stuff, but I've always thought they'd ruin the silhouette. Maybe now I'll have to reconsider. But I'm not letting her take her phone out on practice just so that she can Twitter-stalk her crush.

'Did Jay call tonight?' Erica asks as she gets changed. I root out her phone from the bag with all her stuff in it.

'No calls, but it looks like you got some text messages. Not from him though.'

As Erica scans through her phone, catching up on all the latest gossip from friends that I don't share, I carefully fold up the costume and place it in a shoe box I keep on top of my wardrobe.

'Damn it. He's had my number for over a week now. What the hell is his problem?'

'Why don't you just text him first?'

'Because I'm not meant to have his number! I got it off Karishma, remember? But I know he has mine because Heather heard him ask Nathan for it. Anyway, any hits on the website?'

As well as performing all costume duties, I manage Erica's website. It's not much, more of a holding page really. The idea is that if someone (i.e. the Vigils) wants to get in touch with Erica, they can, without us revealing our personal details. We also regularly check it to see if there are any YouTube videos we can link to, to build up a bit of a fan page. Except that nobody ever gets in touch, and the only hits come from Erica or myself hitting the refresh button.

The big problem is that Erica's too nervous to make a public appearance. She's scared of doing it wrong, and doing it alone, and wants the Vigils to somehow find her first before she's forced to make an early solo debut.

'Nope, nothing,' I reply. She sighs in frustration. I think about telling her that maybe she's just not ready to join the Vigils yet, that she's still so young and maybe she should focus on her exams instead.

But before I even get a chance to mention this, my mum walks in. One day when she comes in completely unannounced, I won't be able to explain what she finds.

'Mum! Why can't you knock?' I yell. She just pouts back at me and rolls her eyes, an expression I'm well aware I'm starting to mimic.

'Lovely to see you too, Lou-Lou,' Mum mocks. Then she turns to Erica. 'You must have come in while I was watching my soaps. I didn't hear a peep!'

'I know you don't like to be disturbed in the evenings, Mrs Kirby,' Erica replies, her voice full of a sweetness I'm unable to muster for my parents. My mum loves Erica. She's the daughter my mum never had – one that's interested in shopping and boys instead of books and sewing. And I know that Erica prefers my parents to her own. But then again, anybody's parents would be preferable to hers. Her dad's not been seen in ages, and to say that Erica and her own mum, Liza, don't get along is something of a massive understatement. So of course when my mum invites Erica downstairs for telly and hot chocolate, Erica practically jumps to follow her, until I remind her that we've still got our homework to do.

'Mum, was there something you actually wanted when you barged in here?' I ask, getting tired of all the niceness.

'I'm putting on a white wash overnight. Got any school shirts that need doing?' She's still putting on that 'perfect-parent' voice because Erica is here, but I find it really irritating.

She even tries to hover and chat after I've given her my bundle of whites, but I remind her that surely one of her programmes must be starting up again soon. Eventually my door closes again and we hear her go downstairs.

'You're way too harsh on her. She just wants to be friends,' Erica says with a pout.

'She just wants to be friends with *you*, you mean,' I counter. 'Seriously, I can't wait until I've done my A levels and can escape to uni. Mum can be rather intense when you have to live with her.'

'Well, at least she's interested.' Erica says this slowly and softly, not meaning to sound confrontational. But she's gently warning me that if I ever start complaining about my mother's coddling, she'll remind me about how

9

lucky I am to be coddled in the first place. I drop the topic. I don't like anything that will lead to discussion about Erica's mum. I never know what to say.

'Maybe I should head home already. I can copy the notes out before I go to bed and give them back to you in the morning before lessons,' Erica says.

'Or maybe, if we work really hard for the next twenty minutes, we can finish up and go and sit downstairs with my parents. They're probably not watching anything good, but you know...there will be hot chocolate...'

'That sounds good,' Erica says, not looking me in the eyes as she smiles. I know how much she loves watching the telly with my folks. She's been coming over to do it for years. And my mum always gives her extra marshmallows in her chocolate too.

'And maybe you'll even get a plastic folder for your notes too. If you're good.'

'Don't say it if you don't mean it,' Erica teases.

'But can I trust you with the good stationery?'

'I'm not going to go all melty on it, if that's what you mean.' She picks up a random piece of paper and rubs it between her fingers. 'See, not even a hint of singe! I am the paragon of chill tonight. Which calls for nothing but the finest of your stationery, my dear Louise!'

Of course she gets the plastic folder. But you can't blame me for being careful, after the Great Melt of last autumn. Nobody wants a repeat of having to pick out the cooled globs of green plastic from my rug. I'm still finding bits of green in that rug now.

When we're ready we go downstairs, and Erica sinks into the sofa next to my mum, which makes her smile. If she could mother the whole world she probably would. I sit next to my dad, who is concentrating on some hardback crime novel and pretending not to be interested in what is happening on the TV. And as she sits there, curled up and comfortable, I think about how awesome it is that we're close like this, and how wonderful things are going to be when the Vigils finally discover her. But not too soon, I secretly hope, because I wouldn't mind Erica being around here for a little while longer. I might not be special, but being so close to someone who is, is nearly as good.

2

I can see Erica out on the terrace, high ponytail bouncing as she laughs with her friends. While she's out there being the perfect social butterfly, I'm in the library shelving books. I say library, but really it's just an open classroom with loads of computers and a book corner. The teachers want us to call it the Information Centre, but nobody does. There's still a wall of shelves holding reference books, but I bet that nobody has touched them in at least a decade. Every now and again Mrs Fraser asks one of the library prefects to give the shelves a good dusting. I always try to find a way to get her to pick me, because the smell of those old and yellowed pages is just amazing. The internet will never smell as good as dusty books.

Erica's talking to a boy, a tall one with floppy hair, and seeing as he's wearing the unofficial sixth-form uniform of jacket and jeans, and not a school uniform, I presume that this is the infamous Jay. I really don't know what Erica sees in him. I mean, sure he has this dark and brooding thing going on, and I can see how some girls would love the fact that he rides a motorbike, but from what I've seen of him in the school corridors, he takes himself far too seriously. Even now, while being fawned over by teenage girls twisting their hair and pouting their lips, he seems so humourless. If he cracked a smile that didn't look slimy and sinister, then maybe I'd support Erica in her pursuit of him. My general rule? If the boy looks as if he could play a pale-faced vampire in a teen movie, it's probably best to stay away.

'You do realise that you just shelved *Lord of the Flies* under Tolkien, right?' Toby reaches around me and pulls out the thin book I've accidentally shelved alongside the epic fantasies, making me jump. I wonder if he realises just how close he is to me right now, because I'm hyperaware.

'Sorry, distracted,' I confess as Erica and her friends move away from the terrace to follow Jay down the hill and out of my line of sight.

Toby and I do lunchtime library duty every Tuesday and Thursday. We don't get paid, but we do get a reference from Mrs Fraser and a chance to escape the dismal purgatory that is the upper-school playground for a couple of hours a week. Having a legitimate reason to be inside during the colder months or when it's raining is pretty cool. But it does mean that we have to work, and Mrs Fraser, who let's not forget gets free labour every day, works us hard. I'm OK because she likes me (I've always rocked the teacher's pet thing). But she absolutely hates Toby for no reason that anyone has ever been able to work out, unless you count the time in Year Seven that he returned a book he had let fall in the bath. But if Mrs Fraser is still holding that against him four years later, well, that's just weird if you ask me.

He's become a best friend of sorts. Not in the same way as Erica, obviously, but in the way that stops me getting desperately lonely at school. It's not that Erica ignores me, or doesn't want me to hang around with her group, but it's always been clear that we spin in different social circles. She has the popular girls, with their skirts hitched up and their perfect hair, and I get the nerds. Or, more precisely, I get Toby, High King of the Nerds. Besides, those girls scare me. They know how to walk and how to talk and I'm just a little mouse next to them. Being around Toby makes me feel cool, and clever, and significant in a way that Erica's friends never do.

This little social setup suited everyone fine until precisely five weeks ago, when the new school year started and Toby returned from the summer holidays taller, without the dappling of acne under his chin and with this new smile thing that makes my tummy flutter. And I try to tell myself to stop it, that it's the same lanky-armed Toby, and he's just my friend, but every now and again, when he gets too close like this, I swear I forget how to form words, or how to move my hands without bashing something over.

'What are you up to this weekend?' he asks, after returning *Lord of the Flies* to 'G' and coming back around to my aisle.

'Not much. Why?' I'm thinking about the costume I have to repair, plus all that homework I have to do twice, plus a knitting pattern I've been dying to try out.

'Me and the guys are going to see that new sci-fi film on Saturday. You can come if you want.'

I look up at Toby, who is making an obvious point of not looking back at me by seeming to be engrossed in the blurb of a sci-fi novel I haven't read. I wonder briefly if he's asking me out, and then I think he's just feeling sorry for me and my lack of a life outside of my bedroom. Suddenly I get annoyed with myself for even thinking that Toby might be interested in me in *that way*, and I find that all I can reply with is a mumbled 'Um . . . maybe?'

I mean, I'll probably, definitely end up saying no. It's not that I don't want to hang out with him and his friends; it's just that Toby and I have never really hung out together outside of a school context, and I'd probably turn into a squirming ball of awkwardness and just embarrass him, or worse, myself, and then I'd have to swap my library shifts, or move schools, or change planets, so that we don't ever see each other ever again. And then what would I do?

He follows me as I move over to the reluctant-reader shelves.

'You know the film is meant to be awesome, right? Like *Back to the Future* for a new generation, except with a future that doesn't seem quite so . . . outdated,' he says.

I'm about to reply with something dazzling and witty, but we're both distracted by lots of whooping and cheering coming from the annexe, a room that sits just off the main library. The heads of all the kids studying in the main room pop up like startled meerkats, desperate to know what's going on. Mrs Fraser stands up behind her desk and indicates for me to investigate. Then she barks at Toby to hurry up with his shelving.

Going into a room full of tall sixth-formers is not really something that I want to be doing. I wonder if there is any chance at all that they'll listen to me if I ask them to be quiet.

Everybody is clustered around one computer terminal, a pack four people deep, all craning to get a view of whatever is on the screen. As I make my way around to see what's happening, there's another jubilant cheer. They're on YouTube, watching the latest Vigil footage from the US team. From what I can see by pushing people's arms out of the way and standing on tiptoes, some scaffolding collapsed on a part-built skyscraper in New York City.

'Has anyone seen Zero yet?' one guy asks. 'He's my favourite!'

'Are you kidding me? Zero's lame. He can't even fly,' says another.

'Says the boy with a poster of Hayley Divine on his wall,' a girl mocks.

Through a small gap between shoulders I can make out the clip, which has been expanded to fill the entire screen. Obviously amateur footage, I'm just in time to see the camera zoom in as Solar appears from a window, clutching onto a hard-hatted builder. Solar's the team leader of the American East Coast Vigils, and apart from being able to fly – the most common superpower of them all – he has the ability to cast intense rays of light from his body at will. He's dressed in his trademark bodysuit of shiny gold, emblazoned with the symbols and patches of his various sponsors, and his face is covered with a golden balaclava, the typical style of the US team. Solar hands the man over to another Vigil, who flies him down to the ground and safety, before going back into the dark web of scaffolding to look for more survivors.

'Wow. They are so epic. And have you seen Solar's arms? I bet he doesn't even have to work out,' a soft-voiced girl sighs.

I head out of the annexe just as the crowd erupts in another roar of excitement and astonishment. I watch the videos same as everybody else, but I prefer to do it at home where I can concentrate on what's happening, and discover how to let them know about Erica. I'm sure that they have their methods, otherwise how does anyone get to become a Vigil? But it can't hurt to be a little proactive in the matter.

'What's going on in there?' Mrs Fraser demands when I reach the library desk.

'Another Vigil video. An American one,' I explain.

'Really?' And suddenly the hardness drops from Mrs Fraser's face. 'Oh, I must see that before it gets taken down!' She bolts into the annexe, adjusting her reading glasses as she goes.

'Was there a time before the Vigils?' I moan at Toby, who's alphabetising some books on a trolley.

'My grandpa tells me stories about what it used to be like, and how everybody thought that it was all those nuclear bombs that started the whole thing off.' Toby doesn't realise that my question is rhetorical. But I don't want to stop him talking, because he has this really specific type of smile when he talks about Vigil stuff. I'm barely listening to what he's saying to be honest – something about the Vigils being wrapped up in conspiracy theories until the advent of cameraphones and social media – I've learned to zone out when he starts giving it the Toby Talk. 'So I guess we're stuck with them. Unless you can figure out a way to stop the internet from happening?'

'I'd be lucky,' I sigh. I think hanging around Erica so much has made me immune to all the excitable hype that surrounds the Vigils. Some days I wish they would all go away and I could have some time off from thinking about them.

'Ever wondered what would happen if one of us turned out to be one of them?' Toby asks.

'What?' I try not to sound too startled.

'I mean, the chance of that happening is next to nothing of course, and even then, the odds against having a power significant enough to put you on the Vigil A-team are just ridiculous, but imagine... What if you woke up one day and could fly? What if you had Deep Blue or the Red Rose on speed-dial? Do you think you'd still have to come to school?'

'Who knows...?'

'Do you think there could be superpeople living among us? Even going to this school?'

'Of course it's possible, but also really unlikely.' I'm thinking very carefully as I talk, but it's not as if Toby would ever actually suspect anything. There's just no way. 'I mean, how could they hide it? Surely we'd know.'

'Still, I think having superpowers would be momentously cool.' He gets a boyish glint in his eye, like a five-year-old thinking about Christmas. 'I'd totally want the X-ray vision. Can you imagine how much fun that would be?'

And there it is. A reminder like a kick to the fluttery parts that he's just another teenage boy with normal teenage-boy thoughts. And boys aren't interested in girls like me. Besides, I know that Toby has all these pictures of the Red Rose on his phone, and it's not as if I'm ever going to look like her.

'You're so pathetic,' I scold, saying it half to him, half to myself.

'Oh, come on. If you could have any superpower, what would it be?' If only he knew just how much I've thought about this.

'Right now, just the power to get through this school year would be enough.' I laugh it off, because what else can I say? That I've dreamed of every possible scenario under the sun? That I watch all the Vigil videos, wondering what it would be like to be one of them? 'Let's get on and finish the shelving. Mrs Fraser's coming back.'

The library empties out. Kids have either gone into the annexe to watch more Vigils footage, or have gone somewhere else to watch the latest action on their phones, because Mrs Fraser has a thing about using them in here.

Out of the window I can see Erica standing just a little way down the hill, gossiping with her friends, talking about the boys they like and the teachers they hate. Jay seems to have disappeared. Erica does such a great job of pretending that she's just like them, better than I could ever manage. It's as if hiding her true self is just another one of her many gifts, in addition to the flying and the flame-throwing. Sometimes I wonder if we'd even be friends if it wasn't for all of that. We were drifting apart before she discovered what she could do, and then she decided to come to me with her secret. If it hadn't have been me, then what? I'd be just another nerd with straight

As and hardly any friends. I bet she doesn't even realise how she saved me.

Then I think about all she's destined for, another star in one of those videos, with her own celebrity-like cult surrounding her. There'll be posters of her on teenagers' walls alongside Hayley Divine, and boys like Toby will moon over her instead of the Red Rose. How will our friendship survive all of that? And then I remember: if our friendship can survive secondary school, it can survive anything.

3

It's dark. And it's cold. My hands are stuffed in my duffel-coat pockets and my scarf is wrapped around my neck so tightly I can barely move my head. To complete this rocking look of human autumn bundle, I'm wearing my favourite bobble hat, one of the first I ever knitted. (And yes, I have knitted more than one. Way more than one.) Erica absolutely hates it, but she can hate all she likes – the terms and conditions of dragging me outside to watch her practise are that she doesn't get to say a thing about what I wear. It's not as if she could ever understand my need for chunky knitwear anyway. She never gets cold.

Erica is up in the air in complete costume, so unless she lights her hands up I can't see her at all. As well as the black catsuit and boots, she's wearing her mask, a black bandit's mask on elastic, and the thick black hairband that covers her forehead as well as keeping her hair away from her face. The look may be a little DIY, but from a distance it does the job really nicely. She still has those holes at her elbows that I need to fix; at the moment they look like the kind of patches that really dorky teachers might wear. Her posture changes when she's in costume. Instead of being Erica Elland, regular if highly popular schoolgirl, she becomes Flamegirl, blue eyes glimmering behind her makeshift mask, as if her fire is lighting them up too.

Sometimes I can hear the whoosh of her flying past me, but it's far too dark and she's far too high up for me to see anything. So I'm left back on the ground, waiting and watching and secretly hoping the evening will end soon so that I can get back to my homework. During the summer evenings we did all kinds of experiments, like testing how fast she could travel, with me holding the stopwatch, but now that the days are getting shorter all I can do is hang around until she gets bored and decides that she wants to go home too.

Suddenly my bobble hat is no longer on my head. It has been plucked into the October air with a familiar swoosh.

'Hey! Erica! Give that back!'

There's a whirling somewhere above me, and I can just about make out a shadow, like a prehistorically large moth, dashing past.

'Erica! That's not funny! You better not set fire to it!'

Just as suddenly as the hat vanished, it's back on my head again, and tugged down past my eyes. When I pull it up to a more comfortable position I see Erica standing before me, hands on her well-honed hips, stomach taut under the black Lycra. Aggravatingly for me, we've discovered that the strength for flying seems to come from the core muscles, so the more Erica flies, the more sickeningly toned her abs become. Flying for her is like super-pilates. Which, if you ask me, is just not fair.

'Will you not go around shouting out my real name, please?' she huffs. 'What if somebody heard you?'

'There's nobody else around, *Erica*.'

'We should get into the habit though. Like, you shouldn't ever call me Erica when I'm in costume. What's the point of having a whole secret identity if you're just going to call me by my real name? And that goes for you too. I'm not going to call you Louise any more when I'm in costume. Just in case somebody figures out who *you* are and gets to me that way.'

'If you start calling me Lou-Lou, like my mother, I will not be happy...'

'I was toying with "L" actually.'

OK. I like it. It makes me feel like a vaguely important character in a Bond film. 'Fine. You can call me "L". But what am I supposed to call you? We can't go on with Flamegirl for ever.'

'Why not?'

'You know I've always thought it was a little corny. It was only ever meant to be temporary, until we came up with something better.'

'Flamegirl' makes me think of Victorian urchins selling newspapers, yelling, 'Read all about it!' on street corners.

'It does what it says on the tin,' says Erica.

We start walking towards the disused train tracks at the bottom of the field, and our favourite hangout, the old tunnel.

'Exactly. People *see* that you can flame-throw, especially when your hands go all flamey. They don't need to be told it as well. It's too obvious.'

'So what would you suggest, L?'

I've been waiting for a good time to have this conversation for ages, because I have an amazing idea. 'I was thinking "Vega" would be an interesting option.'

'Vega? It sounds like an alien.'

'It's the name of a star. One of the brightest fireballs in the sky. I thought it might be fitting.'

'Vega . . . Vega . . .' Erica plays with the word on her lips as we walk. 'I'm not sure. It's a little bit science fiction for my liking.'

'But you have to admit that it's pretty cool for a codename.'

'Maybe. I'm just not convinced that it's *my* codename. Can we just stick to Flamegirl for now? We'll come up with something good sooner or later.'

I suppose it *is* up to Erica to choose. I can't force a name on her. But her frank dismissal of my idea hasn't exactly lightened my mood. As we walk (she walks with me instead of flying when she wants me to go anywhere with her) I think I hear a rustling somewhere behind us.

'What's that?'

'I don't know. A fox? Or a squirrel, maybe.' Erica is obviously not concerned.

I make her stop and stand perfectly still so that I can listen more carefully. Nothing but the wind blowing through trees and the distant traffic from the A-road that runs past this field.

'See? Nothing. Now come on. The sooner we get to the tunnel, the sooner we can get you home.' She tugs me along. I'm still craning to hear whatever might be behind us.

'Have you ever thought about what would happen if anyone followed us?'

'Don't be silly. Nobody comes here at night. Not even the weirdos.'

We're walking a little faster now. I can't shake the feeling that somebody is watching us. Maybe I'm just antsy because of the cold and Erica's name rejection. I've always thought that Flamegirl was a name a four-year-old would come up with.

The tunnel is our special place. The Vigils may have their top-secret hideouts, but we have the crumbling remains of a railway viaduct. Apart from being where Erica and I started testing out her powers, it's also the place we come to when we want to get a bit of distance from the world. Erica tends to use it for that more than I do. When she has a massive bust-up with her mum and doesn't want to bother me, where else can she go? The tunnel is a great cavernous hole lined with bare bricks and filled with weeds, which we've managed to tame back over the years. Once upon a time, trains would have rumbled overhead as they headed to and from London, but the line was abandoned long before I was born.

As soon as we get there, Erica zooms over with her feet off the ground, flying fancy loops in the tunnel and moving in a way that makes me think of a shiny black dragonfly, hands glowing with flames so that the bricks light up a warm ceramic bronze. I settle down on the old bench we moved in here to make the space more comfortable for those of us that don't fly. But I'm still feeling too cold and bored to get properly comfy. I huddle my knees up to my chest anyway.

'So what was it you were so desperate to show me?' I ask, trying my hardest to push back a yawn.

Erica comes towards me, still not letting her feet touch the ground. She pulls off her mask and hairband so that I can see her face clearly, and I put them safely in the rucksack I'm carrying around that contains all her stuff. Her eyes are intense and excited, and the edges of her mouth tip upwards in a mischievous curl.

'OK, so, you know how I heat up?' she starts.

'Yep...'

'Well, it got me thinking about how far I could push that. I'm not talking about the fire or the flames, but just the heat.'

'Right…'

'So, OK, watch this!'

She reaches for a stick near my feet and hands it to me to hold for her. Then she rubs her right thumb against her middle and forefingers – just that slight friction is enough to conjure a flame. Erica plays with it for a bit, as if captivated by her own magic, working the flame so that it grows brighter and hotter. She reaches out her burning hand and sets fire to the stick. It's only a small flame, but still, I'm not the superhuman one, so I hold it out from me at a safe distance.

'Be careful, and let me know if you start to get too hot, OK?' Erica warns as she hovers upwards and back to the far side of the tunnel. She holds out her hands towards the stick, towards me.

The strangest thing happens. I can feel a wave of heat flowing towards me, and then another, and another, steady as a heartbeat. The heat is pouring off Erica, and as she focuses, the flaming stick in my hands flares hotter and brighter.

'Woah! That's new!' I exclaim, dropping the stick to the ground when it gets too hot for me to hold onto any more.

Erica brings her hands back down, turning off the

pulse, and the flare dies down until the stick is just smouldering in the dirt. I stamp it out with my boot.

'So it feels a little unfocused at the moment,' Erica says, a little out of breath from the exertion.

'Yeah, it was like a heat tsunami coming right at me! What do we call this? A heat wave?'

'I don't know, but it's definitely cool, right? But it's like I reach a certain distance, and my focus goes. I want it to be like a concentrated laser-heat-beam thing. Point, focus and BOOM! Once I train myself to get more specific I could do all sorts of things, like I could warm up your tea while you're holding it, or I could totally fry what's left of Mr Scott's hair from the back of the classroom!'

'That's right, Flamegirl, think big!' I chide. 'But also, what about the more practical stuff? Like burning away ice from roads and pavements?'

'Or overheating Lisa Broom's car when she parks it in the teachers' section instead of the sixth-form car park?'

'Or burning away clouds during a rain storm?'

'Or heating my uncle's outdoor pool?'

'Erica, this is awesome,' I say, biting my tongue rather than pointing out that she's thinking a little shallow, because I know that she's only having fun. I think being trivial and funny about her powers is her way of not having to think about all the big and important stuff. I also suspect she does it to wind me up.

'I knew you'd be impressed! Now let's go home.'

I reach into the rucksack and pull out Erica's coat, a light one that she doesn't need for warmth, but more to cover up her costume as we walk back out of the park. As she gets herself back in order I wander towards the tunnel mouth, peering out into the suburban quiet. I still can't shake the feeling that somebody is watching us. If there was anyone out in the field, they would have had a clear line of sight into the tunnel, which Erica has just lit up like a Christmas tree. I concentrate, trying to hear past the whistling breeze. Nothing. But...I suppose it could just be the urban foxes in the bushes. I mean, who would even know to follow us all the way out here?

'Still hearing things?' Erica asks me.

'Not exactly. I just have this feeling.'

'Stop stressing. We're not being watched. Now let's get you home, missy! Fancy a lift over the field?'

She comes up behind me and hooks me up under the arms, so that I'm dangling as she flies.

'Erica!' I yell. 'Put me down!'

'Nope! Not until you stop calling me that!'

'But you're the one that just said that there's nobody here! And anyway, you're not even technically in costume any more!'

'You've got to get into the habit. Right now I'm Flamegirl! Get used to it!'

Despite all her capabilities, Erica doesn't have super-strength. She heaves me upwards as she flies higher, painfully yanking my arms half out of their sockets. If she drops me now I'll be nothing but a bobble-hatted splat on the grass.

'Put me down! It hurts!'

'Call me Flamegirl first.'

'Seriously? Put me down, Flamegirl!'

'Say please.'

'PLEASE!'

She huffs as she lowers me, finally letting go just as my feet meet the ground. We're nearly on the other side of the field, close to where it opens up to the playground and the tennis courts. We have to go through the park; although the main gates will be closed by now, there's a gap in the fence that we've been using for years that comes out really close to Erica's house. I roll my shoulders, adjusting the rucksack, and massage my arms as they ease back into their natural positions.

'You're so grumpy tonight,' Erica moans. 'It's no fun.'

'Well, I just don't appreciate being armpitted without any warning, thank you very much.'

'*Please*, you weren't even two metres off the ground.'

'How was I meant to know that? It's dark!'

We walk in silence towards the park gates. I hate it when she goes into Excited-Child Mode. It's as if she forgets that anyone else has feelings. I mean, of course I'm excited for her, discovering a new side to her powers. It's amazing, fantastic even, but then she just doesn't calm down about it. It's like she gets an adrenaline-pumped energy high, a sudden need to do something big and daring, and sometimes (especially on cold October evenings when there is homework still outstanding) I'm just not up for playing.

By the time we reach the gap in the fence I'm feeling rotten, like I've ruined her birthday party. I turn towards her to say something, but can't think of anything that would melt this frostiness.

Erica crawls through the gap first, then holds it back for me (she won't fly over the fence in case she's spotted by any passers-by). The whole time there's still that sensation, like an itch between my shoulder blades, that we're not alone. It's not a pleasant feeling. I turn round one more time before I exit the park, expecting to see someone there. But there's nobody. I catch Erica's raised eyebrow as she waits for me to crawl through and I wonder if she's in a mature enough place right now to notice if anything's wrong or out of place. Probably not.

'Jay has a bike like that,' Erica comments, nodding her head over to where a motorbike is parked across the road.

I was hoping that we might have been able to get through this evening without a single Jay mention, but apparently not. We're at the stage in her infatuation where everything reminds her of him: songs, films and now, apparently, random vehicles in the street.

'He'll text me soon, right?' she asks me.

'Of course he will.' My voice is on autopilot. Frequent affirmations of Jay's imagined intentions have become rather routine lately. 'Come on, Flamegirl, let's go home.'

4

I hate it when we argue. It's not like we have huge bust-ups, but it's times like these, when she's in Excited-Child Mode and I can't seem to suppress my Sensible Voice, that I think about why it's getting harder and harder for us to click the way we used to. Maybe it's just a part of growing up, but we seem to disagree more than we agree, and because she's the one with the superpowers, I'm always the one who ends up backing down. She finds ways to make it up to me, like when she spent a science lesson making me a bouquet of twisted-up melted biros (she claimed she used the Bunsen burner, but I know better), or when she burnt out a clump of Annabel Hopkin's hair after she was mean to me. Erica went in with her fingers after saying that she thought Annabel's hair was really pretty and wanted to feel how soft it was, and then just one quick-burn flash was enough for her to bring away a substantial lock. Erica suggested that she get new straighteners, and Annabel ran to the toilets in tears, after we both categorically denied that we could smell burning.

And yet it seems like it's getting harder and harder to feel the fun.

When this whole thing started it felt like we were forming our own secret club, just like the kind we used to invent when we were back in primary school, complete with special codes and secret handshakes. Only then we were in Year Eight, nearly thirteen, and it had been a while since we had spent any real time together. I don't like to dwell on it too much, but after we got to secondary school it seemed like I didn't really matter to Erica any more. She found new friends, friends with fashion sense, who were interested in boys and hanging out at the shopping centre for absolutely no reason. I found my people too, but really they were just people to sit with in class and talk with at breaktime. When I saw her laughing with her new friends, I knew that what I had wasn't the same.

Then all of a sudden we had a shared secret, and things were back to how I remembered them.

We had barely spoken in more than a year. One evening, she came round to my house. It was dark and raining. I remember the rain because it was sizzling and evaporating off Erica's super-heated skin, frizzing her hair and creating a fuzzy aura around her. It was my mum who opened the door. She must have presumed that Erica had had another bustup with her mum (this wasn't long after Erica's dad had left, and she and Liza had started arguing a lot), so she didn't ask any questions. Mum was oblivious to our growing distance in secondary school, so she just let Erica go straight up to my room.

When she got there, she slammed my door closed behind her, rocking my window pane. She froze, looking at me with her mouth just moving, as if she was trying to figure out what to say and losing the words before they could form. Her breathing was fast and ragged, and for a long moment I was frozen too, watching her with my pen in my hand (because obviously I was doing homework at the time).

Drops of moisture were being toasted away by the heat from her skin, and it soon became so humid in my room that I had to open my window, even though it was raining, for some fresh air.

'What's going on?' I asked.

Right there, away from the social rules of secondary school, we were like sisters again. There was no need for formalities, no time for me to get excited by the fact that she had come to me in her time of need and not one of her new, silly schoolfriends. In my room we were as we'd always been.

'Something's happening to me,' Erica whimpered. 'I don't understand it.'

I stared at her. Something was definitely happening, and I wanted to reassure her in my most sensible voice that it was just a part of growing up, and that maybe puberty was just taking a particularly horrible toll. But the frightened glisten in her eyes told me that whatever was going on involved far more than temperamental hormones.

'Do you need me to come with you to the hospital?' I asked, and suddenly felt very stupid for asking. Why would she be here with me if the hospital was even an option?

'Look!' Erica held out her palm, and the steam rose from her fingertips like tiny ghosts. 'I'm hot. I'm hot all over, and it's like this burning is happening really deep inside and I don't know how to make it stop!'

'When did it start?' I ask.

'I don't know. It's been going on a while, but it's getting worse. I mean, I've heard about old ladies getting hot flushes and stuff and at first I just thought it was like that. I even booked a doctor's appointment, but that's another week and a half away. And anyway, it's different now. I know it's not a hot flush. I'm sure of it. It's like my whole body is actually making the heat, not just feeling hot. What's happening to me?'

I stepped towards her, cautious as though I was approaching a skittish animal, and reached out and took hold of one of her hands. It was boiling, so hot that I couldn't even keep hold of it for more than a few moments. I thought about getting the thermometer from the bathroom, but that might make Erica feel like she was a science experiment or something. Besides, it would only confirm what was already abundantly clear: Erica was really, really hot right now.

'See?' Erica cried, then hushed herself, probably scared that my mum would come in. 'What's going on? What *is* this?'

We needed to cool her down right away. I ran a bath, switching the cold tap all the way up. I didn't even touch the hot tap. Then I ran downstairs, told my mum that Erica was staying the night and that her mum had said that it was OK (I knew that my mum wouldn't check – she preferred to avoid contact with Liza as much as possible), then snuck into the kitchen and grabbed all the bags of frozen veg. I figured, as long as the bags weren't open, I could sneak them back in the freezer again afterwards.

Erica was waiting in the bathroom when I got back upstairs, every inch of her flaming red. Forgetting our teenage awkwardness in the face of an obvious emergency, I took her clothes from her as she finished getting undressed and then held her hand as she got into the bath. She yelped as she stepped in, and as she settled I sat myself back against the bathroom door in case my parents decided that they wanted to come in (the lock had been broken for years. Still is, in fact). I told Erica to breathe as she relaxed into the cold water. I tried to think of something else, anything else, that I could do. At this point neither of us had any real clue about what was actually going on. I wondered whether I should call an ambulance.

The icy-cold water, along with the floating bags of frozen vegetables, seemed to be calming her. Her skin was returning to its usual Erica-colour and I decided that an ambulance wouldn't be necessary. Maybe this was all a bizarre one-off.

'There have been dreams as well,' Erica said. 'Dreams about heat and fire and burning buildings. I'm running through the buildings, or sometimes flying. In fact, a lot of flying. Flying through corridors, flying up staircases, flying down the middle bit in stairwells, with flames all around me. It's like, every night.'

'Are you particularly stressed out about anything right now?' I remember instantly biting my tongue after I asked that, remembering her parents' split, which had happened only the summer before.

'Loads of kids go through divorce. It's not a big deal,' she said with a sigh. 'I mean, my mum and I aren't getting along right now, but so what? Doesn't mean that I should be heating up. But there is other stuff too. There's this guy, Duncan, but Heather also likes him, and she's throwing this party next weekend and they're blatantly going to get together. He doesn't even notice me.'

'Still doesn't sound like anything more than usual-person stress.' Usual-Erica stress, I added mentally.

We chatted for about an hour as she cooled down in my bath. To be honest, she did most of the talking. I found out so much about her friends and all their ways and quirks, which was cool, because they were pretty much the celebrities of our school and I was never going to hear this stuff from anybody else. She never asked me about my friends, but I wouldn't have had much to tell. Listening to Erica rattle on, and then go off on bizarre tangents about music and fashion, was surprisingly fun – it was as if a world that had been silent for ages suddenly had all this colourful noise.

Eventually, when we figured that she had cooled down enough, Erica got out of the bath. Then she took a look in my mirror. 'Oh my God – my hair!'

Instead of hair, she pretty much had a halo of blonde frizz. I couldn't help it, I laughed, and after the initial horror, Erica started laughing too. I let her lie on my bed in my fluffiest and therefore most comfortable dressing gown while I took what would soon become my usual position at my desk.

'Do you remember how we first became friends?' Erica asked me. She wanted to tell the story. She loves it like it's our very own creation myth.

It had been years since I last heard it. We were actually born just days apart – I was early, she was late – but we were both due on the same day, 4 May. If the universe had gone to plan, our mothers would have met in the maternity ward and we would have been friends since the moment we were born. As it happens, we ended up meeting at nursery, and were inseparable from the outset.

'We should have been twin sisters,' Erica said wistfully, as if recalling the Happily Ever After of a fairy tale.

It wasn't long after that we figured out what was really going on. Erica kept having the 'flushes', but every time I suggested going to the doctor she would refuse. Thank goodness for her embarrassment, because if she had presented to a doctor and they had realised what was happening before we did, then things would have turned out a lot differently. I don't suppose doctor-patient confidentiality extends to superpowers. And then there's always the crazy fear that some person with bad intentions could discover you before the good guys do, or that your secret identity could get exposed too soon. It's perfectly fine for the really well-known superheroes to reveal their true identities. All their sponsorship means they can afford the security for their friends and family. But for a newbie it can be a career-ending catastrophe, as well as dangerous for the superhero and the people around them. But we didn't have everything figured out back then. Maybe I had an inkling, more like a wild hope, and maybe Erica did too, but we never spoke about it.

Erica would come over to my house nearly every day after school. I asked if her schoolfriends minded, and she said that she was having a massive argument with Heather anyway and couldn't be bothered to hang out with them at the moment. Inside I was glowing. I suspected it wasn't just because of Heather that Erica was choosing me. She could trust me in a way that she couldn't trust them. We *were* like sisters.

She told me about her dreams, which were growing in intensity.

'It's like I can't even close my eyes without seeing flames now,' she said. 'All the time, the burning, and the light and the heat. Did I tell you I found scorch marks on my sheets the other day? It was so embarrassing! Burned right through to the mattress. I can't let my mum find out. And I can't go anywhere any more without an iced drink to cool me down! It's so stupid. I can be doing almost nothing at all and then, *wham!* I'll feel the blushing and my pulse will race and then there's all the sweating!'

The thing that bothered Erica more than anything else at this stage was the sweating. She was dressing as light as she could, but as the evenings got darker earlier it started to look strange that she wouldn't wear a coat or tights with her school uniform. People were asking questions, and the more she worried, the hotter she got. She had to wear her hair in a high ponytail because the nape of her neck would get so wet, and she got through nearly a whole can of deodorant a day. Those were hard, horrible times. We'd have secret meetings at lunchtime, where I would supply her with extra body spray and listen to all her fears and worries (mostly about what boys would think), and then she'd meet me at my house after school, where she'd lie on my bed on top of towels and I'd place packs of frozen peas on her boiling tummy as if they were hot-water bottles and all she had were the cramps.

Then there was the spark.

Naturally the spark was her mother. Erica hated her mother, and was convinced that her mother hated her back. She's probably still convinced about this, but I just can't believe it. Call me the naive, bubble-wrapped daughter of happily-married childhood sweethearts, but I just can't believe that any mother can hate her daughter. Not really. Try telling Erica that though. Liza had been just a teenager when she'd had Erica, and had married Erica's father in haste to appease her conservative family. It didn't work out, but they'd stuck together for as long as they could. I think arguing is the only form of communication that Erica understands when it comes to family members. Normal conversations are saved for when she comes round to my house.

'I don't even know what we were yelling about in the end, you know? I think it started because she thought my skirt was too short, and even though I had leggings on and you couldn't even see anything at all, she still wanted me to change. And I said something about it not being my fault that she was so out of touch with fashion, and then she screamed and said, IT IS YOUR FAULT! And I screamed back at her, because, you know, I'M SORRY THAT I WAS EVEN BORN! And then she gave me this look, this look that told me that she hated me, that same look she used to give Dad in the end, and then something just *popped*. It's just like the hot flushes, except that it feels more urgent, like a charge going right through my fingers that I absolutely have to get out of me.'

She had got scared and knew that she had to get out of the house, so texted me to meet her at the park.

I couldn't even stand close to her because of all the hot, angry heat that was pouring off her, pulsing with intensity.

'I just can't believe her!' she was yelling.

I guided us both away from the main part of the park, past the playground, and out towards the fields, where I knew there would be fewer people.

'It was like she wished that she had never had me or something! It was horrible! But do you think she'd let me go and live with Dad? No. Because she hates his family too and she says that he'd have no time for me between his job and his new girlfriend, and I was like, well, at least the time I would spend with him would be meaningful! And then I don't know how many times I have to hear her call me a petulant brat, but there you go. I thought her face was going explode with it!'

'I'm sorry,' I offered, not sure what else to say.

Her temperature was rising even further as she recalled the argument, her fists white with tension. And then, with one final, exasperated sigh, it happened. It broke the air like a summer thunderstorm.

Erica's hands were on fire. She held both of them out in front of her, whimpering with panic. She moved them slowly, turned them over, staring at the yellow-orange flames.

'What is this? What is it?' she was whispering, almost too scared to speak.

'Just keep calm, OK? Try and breathe slowly.' I said it like I knew what I was talking about. I wished I did.

'I'm on fire, Lou, I'm on fire!'

'Does it hurt?'

'What?' She looked at me like this hadn't even occurred to her. 'No, actually. It doesn't hurt at all.'

'OK then.' We both stood in the field, mesmerised by her flaming hands.

'Why doesn't it hurt though? Shouldn't it be hurting?'

'I don't know. But presumably not hurting is a good thing. Maybe this is what all those crazy weeks of flushes have been about? Maybe it's all been leading up to *this*?'

'Well, that could make sense. But...'

'But what?'

'But *how the hell do I turn it off*?'

'I don't know!'

'I must be able to turn it off! How do I turn it off?' The flames grew larger as she became more agitated.

It was then that I remembered the old tunnel we used to explore when we were younger. I led her there, certain that it would be deserted. I worked on trying to keep her calm, realising that if stress made the flames bigger, then it was likely that relaxing would make them smaller. Sure enough, we managed to get the fire down to nothing but a dull glow, until finally, after lots of breathing, Erica wiped at her hands and the flames were gone. I held her hands afterwards, looking for the burns, but there was nothing. The skin might have been a little dry, but other than that, her hands had gone back to normal.

We finally knew what was happening. We were starting to understand what Erica was capable of. She was like those superheroes you saw on the news, working alongside the coastguard and the fire brigade and the police. The Vigils, who up until that point had been no more important to us than the actors in my mum's beloved soaps, or whoever was number one in the charts, were suddenly within reach. And it was exciting. Not, dressing-up-to-go-to-a-party exciting, but proper life-changing exciting. Things were changing, and everything that had seemed so important just the day before now became silly and juvenile.

Over the next few days, the Vigils became all Erica could talk about.

'I have to practise. I have to get really good and then the Vigils will have to have me on their A-team,' she would say. 'I want to be ready when they find me, you know?'

I did know, and I understood. For the first time in her life, Erica could see a family and a home of her own.

5

We don't usually go to Erica's house after a practice. We either leave each other at the park gate, or, most often, Erica comes back to mine for some exciting homework catch-up time. So when Erica casually suggests, after her mini-speech about the awesomeness of Jay's motorbike, that we go to hers for a change, I'm a bit too stunned to say anything in protest. It's not that I don't want to go to her house; the house itself is perfectly all right. Just another Identikit suburban semi, like mine. It's Erica's mum, Liza, that I'm worried about. They have the kind of screaming rows I've only ever seen before in soap operas. Raging, door-slamming, emotionally charged arguments that don't let up despite there being company present. More than once Erica has had to dash round to my place for an emergency ice-cold bath so that she doesn't burn her whole house down. I'm socially awkward on my best days, so just imagine what I'm like when I'm around both of them.

'Don't worry, she's not in,' Erica says as she unlocks the front door.

I'm not surprised that she's noticed my reticence. I'm practically twitching with dread on her driveway.

'Where is she?' I ask, trying to sound nonchalant.

'Doing an evening course. Business something or other. Apparently I zapped all her potential the moment I came along and ruined her life. It's only now that she feels confident enough to go out and learn stuff. That's what she actually said – can you believe it?' We dump our coats and shoes in the hallway and head up the stairs. 'It's like she blames me for her entire personality, but she must have had one before she had me, so I wonder who she blamed it on then.'

'Well, at least she's doing something about it now,' I offer. 'And if she's going to be so busy studying, then that must ease things on you.'

'You'd think, wouldn't you?'

I'm not sure that going back to Erica's house tonight is the best idea. I'm working too hard to fight the tired and irritable mood, which, coupled with Erica's hyperaware-ness when she steps into her house, makes for an uncomfortable energy. I know how much she hates her home. So I'm hovering awkwardly in her bedroom, wondering what to do. Does she want me to stay? I've still got my scarf wrapped around my neck, and I'm regretting taking my shoes off when I came in.

Erica starts to get changed, handing her costume over to me so that I can keep it safe. We do this partly in case her secret identity is discovered and someone raids her home looking for proof, and partly because if Erica keeps anything important at her house, there's a good chance it will be found by her mother at some point. The thought of Liza knowing about Erica's powers is enough to make me shudder.

'You can sit down, you know,' Erica says, and all of a sudden I feel monumentally stupid for just standing around, so I let myself flop back in Erica's beanbag chair and reach for her laptop.

'Looks like Hayley Divine wore a nearly see-through dress to a club opening.' Erica's homepage is the main Vigil gossip site, so a picture of Hayley Divine in another trademark barely-there dress comes up full size on the screen the moment I've loaded up her browser, along with all the pop-up advertising for Vigil merchandise and sponsors. 'And apparently Zero has been out on another date with that girl who won the Best Supporting Actress Oscar.'

'Big wow. He eats celebrities for breakfast. And I hear he's planning on playing himself in his own film biopic.'

'Well, at least he'd be able to do his own stunts.'

I think about what it would be like to switch on my computer and see Erica there, in some designer outfit, on the arm of some famous film star. I'm not really sure that I'd like it.

I notice that Erica has bookmarked a page called the International Superhero Name Database. Clicking on the link reveals a registry of every superhero I've ever heard of, and some I haven't. Laid out in columns and rows, the names are cross-checked with apparent powers and country of residence. Much of the information is blocked for public viewing and requires a password, which I suppose makes sense, for security reasons.

'Is this, like, a proper government registry or something?' I ask, surprised that I haven't come across it before.

'It's not official. I think there's a fanboy in Brazil looking after it. But it's pretty cool, right? Comprehensive, I mean.'

Erica comes up behind me and leans on the back of the beanbag. It's not really big enough for two people, but she finds a way of draping herself across the back of it that isn't too awkward for either of us. Me being a rather small person makes things a little easier too.

'I was looking up names,' Erica says, as though she's revealing some big secret. 'Not that I think there's anything wrong with Flamegirl, but I just, you know, wanted to check all the options.'

'But you realise that maybe Flamegirl isn't exactly ideal?' I'm tentative, because I don't want her going all pissy on me again for saying that I don't like the name. I'm a bit nervous about this whole conversation actually, and if Erica gets even slightly hot and bothered, then we could find ourselves on a big melty blob instead of a beanbag.

'I know you don't like it,' Erica says. 'But it suits for now, doesn't it? And look, nobody else has listed it yet, so I was thinking of registering it before anybody else gets in there first.'

I crane my neck around so that I can give Erica a look.

'What?' she says, defensive.

'It's just a big step, that's all.'

'But I wouldn't do it without talking to you first. And I'm not even sure if it's the right time yet.'

Erica's expecting me to say that of course it's the right time, but my silence makes her shift behind me.

'I know what you really think about the whole Vigils thing,' she says, not in an accusing way, but still in a way that makes me think very carefully about what I say next.

'It's just that, you're still so young. And what if it's not for you? Being a Vigil isn't just about the parties and the clothes. You're going to have to do the scary stuff too.'

'You know I know that . . .'

'Plus we have exams this year, and haven't you thought about college? Or even university? You do have other options, you know.'

'But then sometimes I think that I lost all my options when I discovered that I can fly,' Erica says. 'The Red Rose was fourteen when she was made a member of the Vigils. And Quantum was sixteen. And it's not as if anything happens in this town that allows me to really show off my abilities. I'll never be ready unless something actually happens. And what's the other option? Stand on the fourth plinth in Trafalgar Square and set fire to the lions?'

I turn to look up at Erica, whose face has started to get blotchy with emotion. I take a mental note of everything in her room that might be flammable.

'What's the point of all this practising if I'm just going to stay in this town and do A levels? Joining the Vigils has been my dream ever since I found out what I can do. And yes, the fame and fortune and living in a mansion or whatever would be nice, but I know about the other part too. And of course it's really scary. But if I just hang around here and wait for real danger to strike, am I ever going to be ready?'

We're stuck in another one of those horrid silences again. We really must stop having these. Especially in her house when Liza could come home any minute.

'And seriously, is Flamegirl really such a bad name?' Erica's the one to break the silence while shifting her position behind me.

'Well, you can also fly. Why don't we call you Flygirl?' I suggest.

'Because there's already a Flygirl working on the South African Vigil team.' She reaches around me and scrolls down the computer screen. 'See? She's registered right there between the Feline and Frostfire.'

'Well, has anyone taken Vega yet?' I scroll and see that they haven't.

'I told you, I don't like that name.'

'I know, I know. But as your manager, I'm allowed to strongly suggest it. It's cool – and modern, I think.'

'It sounds like what somebody might call an asteroid.'

'It's not an asteroid. It's a star.'

'Give up on it, Lou. I don't like it. Let's just register Flamegirl and get it over and done with. Who knows – maybe the Vigils check this website, and then somebody will come knocking in the morning.'

'Of course. Because that's precisely how international teams of superhuman crime fighters and rescuers work. They search the websites made by fanboys.'

Although, to be honest, that could very well be how they work. We've read up on countless theories about how the Vigils go recruiting, from online spying and phone-tapping to the crazy notion that they've got some psychic working for them whose sole purpose is to root out potential superheroes. The truth is, how they actually operate is as closely guarded a secret as where they're based, or who's really in charge. And if anybody is going to get to the root of the operation and suss them out, it's hardly going to be a couple of teenage girls.

Erica's phone pings on her bed, and she clambers around me so that she can reach it.

'Oh. Em. Gee.'

'What?' I don't really care who's messaged her and what they're saying, because chances are it's something to do with her other friends, but I know that if I don't feign interest, Erica's only going to get annoying about it.

'You won't believe who's messaged me!'

'Who?' OK, so it looks like she's going to get annoying about it anyway.

'No, seriously, guess! You won't believe it!'

'But if I won't believe it, then how am I meant to guess?'

'Sometimes, Lou-Lou, you are just absolutely no fun.' A dramatic pause so that she can glare at me for a bit. 'It's Jay! Jay has sent me a message! Jay has FINALLY sent me a message!'

'Oh. Yay?'

'He wants to know what I'm doing this weekend. *What are you doing this weekend?* Is he asking me out? This is so exciting!'

I move so that Erica can get up properly, and she dashes over to her wardrobe to look at her clothes. She's already planning her outfit before even replying to him. Seriously?

'Aren't you going to message him back?' I ask.

'Of course I am!' Erica giggles. 'But not right away. Never right away. I'll probably wait until tomorrow to reply. Or whatever.'

'So then in the meantime maybe we should read those chapters for English.'

'Or you can read them and tell me what happens, and I can find something to wear?' She's laughing as if she's joking, but I know that really she's not.

'You're not the only one who's got plans with a boy this weekend, you know.'

I don't know why I say it. I really don't. I wasn't going to say anything about it at all. I thought I could get away with pretending that Toby hadn't asked me, and then maybe he'd forget too, and then we could just go about our lives as usual. But I feel like pushing back against her for once. There's something about her obsession with this Jay guy, and the way that she's blown off the name thing *and* my suggestion of knuckling down with the homework. There was also the armpitting earlier. My shoulders have definitely not forgotten about that yet.

Erica's staring at me with her mouth open. So now I'm going to have to tell her that Toby asked me to go to the cinema – with him and his friends, not with him singular – and it definitely isn't a date situation, however much I'd like it to be. It also means having to admit that I might possibly have some kind of feelings for Toby. She's still staring at me, waiting for me to say something, so I try to deflect by shrugging and looking back at her laptop.

'Oh no, you don't,' Erica demands. 'You can't just say something like that and expect to get away with it!'

'It was a mistake! I didn't mean to say anything!' I insist.

'Oh my God, you are so blushing!'

'I'm not!' Although of course I am. I can feel the heat burning over my jawline and up my cheeks.

'Is it Toby? Did Toby finally ask you out?'

'He didn't ask me out, OK? He just said that he was going to the cinema with some friends this weekend, and asked if I wanted to come too. As friends. Definitely as friends.'

'But this is perfect!' Erica cries.

'How exactly is this perfect?'

'I can tell Jay that I want to go to the cinema and then I can meet you there, and you can meet Jay and finally see what an amazing guy he is, and I can help you with Toby. Perfect, right?'

'Are you trying to turn all this into a double-date situation?'

'Nope. Nu-uh. Definitely not.'

I'm not so sure. But Erica's smiling, and she looks nearly as happy as she does when her hands do their full-powered flamey thing. I decide that the best way to get out of this is to roll my eyes and smile back at her, because it's only Wednesday after all, which means that there's plenty of time to get out of this whole thing before the weekend comes around.

'Erica!' shrieks a voice from downstairs. Well, there goes her good mood.

'Damn it. She's back already. Want me to walk you home?'

As we go down the stairs I can hear cupboards slamming in the kitchen, and I'm hoping that I can put my shoes and coat back on and get out of the house before Liza notices me.

'Erica? Did you finish the milk?' Liza calls.

'I haven't had any since breakfast,' Erica calls back.

'But did you finish the milk at breakfast?'

'I don't know!'

'But if you did, do you think that maybe you should have picked some more up on your way home?'

'Sorry, I forgot.' Erica makes stupid faces at me while we get our coats on.

I peer round the banister and see Liza in the kitchen. She's rubbing her forehead with a shaking hand, and with the other pouring the contents of a bottle of wine into a coffee mug. I quickly turn back round in case she sees me spying.

'It's just that I get home, and I can't even have a cup of tea, you know?'

'Mum, I'm going to walk Louise home, OK?'

Liza emerges from the kitchen with one arm folded across her chest, the other one holding the mug. She looks like an older, slightly shrunken version of Erica, except that her hair is pulled back in a shabby ponytail.

'Oh, hi, Louise. How are you?'

'I'm good, Mrs Elland,' I say, immediately getting nervous about whether I should have used her married name, or just called her Liza, or just not said her name at all.

'Well . . .' If she's bothered by my gaffe, it doesn't show on her face – 'perhaps, Erica, you could have told me that you had a friend over before I started screaming my guts out.'

'But it's just Louise,' Erica reasons.

'We'll have a chat about this when you get home, OK?' And with that Liza saunters back into the kitchen, taking long sips from her mug.

At first Erica doesn't say anything as we walk. She keeps her hands stuffed in her pockets and her eyes down to the pavement. 'So tell me about Toby then,' she sighs. I know that she wants distracting from thinking about having to go back to her house, so I'm willing to play along with her for a bit.

'There's nothing much to tell. He just mentioned that he was going to the cinema on Saturday and asked if I wanted to come along.'

'He so blatantly likes you.'

'I really don't think so.'

'Boys aren't that scary, you know. You shouldn't get so embarrassed about hanging out with them. Even if this doesn't work out, it's not the end of the world. I mean, look at me and Stuart. And Tall Josh. And remember that whole debacle with Duncan?'

I want to remind Erica that of course she doesn't have any problems getting boys to like her. She's beautiful and popular and all she has to do is strut down a school corridor to get a legion of potential boyfriends. It seems so easy for her. She likes a guy, and *boom*: he texts her asking her out. It's definitely not so easy for me. Not when you're sure that you don't look quite right, and nothing comes out of your mouth without an awkward splutter.

'You should text Jay back tonight,' I offer. 'It'll make you feel better.'

'You forget that I'm playing the long game here. He made me wait for ages, remember, so I can't text him back until at least twelve hours have passed. Otherwise I'll seem too eager.'

'But you *are* eager.'

'Yes, but he can't know that!' She's smiling again at least.

When we reach my driveway I invite Erica in for hot chocolate, but she declines and shifts her feet.

'Mum'll only get more angry if I avoid her,' she explains.

'Call me later if you want, OK? Any time.'

Erica replies by wrapping me up in a giant, hot hug. She lets me go and I head on up the path to my house. When I get to my door I turn to watch as she trudges down the road. Even though I know exactly what she's capable of, and how much power she has, I can't help but think that right now she just looks like a scared and lonely little girl.

Everybody has a favourite Vigil. It's what kids in the playground ask after finding out your favourite colour, or what you want to be when you grow up. Allegiance to one hero or another denotes your tribe, your social standing, your politics. Intellectuals tend to follow Deep Blue, with his staggering mental powers; headstrong gallivanting types are drawn to Quantum and his intense physical prowess; and arty liberals are more likely to trail the exploits of Oria, a Vigil who can control and manipulate moods. Who you follow says as much about you as how you wear your hair, or what blogs you read. There's a whole pantheon of modern deities out there to worship, who come complete with collectible pencil cases, lunch-boxes and matching duvet covers.

Not that I let myself get caught up in all that.

I don't like to think of myself as a fangirl. Following Vigil stuff is purely business, for the sake of my best friend. Yes, I might be spending my Friday evening downloading the latest Vigil footage while sewing elbow patches onto a superhero costume, but this is work. Plus, I can't lie, I'm desperate to know how they operate and what they do, if only so that I can prepare Erica for it. I mean, there really is no doubt that Erica will be joining the Vigil ranks some day, and when it comes I want her to be ready. I'm not exactly sure what I'm looking for when I'm going through all the clips. I just hope that something might stand out, some clue as to who they really are, and how we might contact them.

I admit I really enjoy it. Everything that Erica does and achieves, I feel like I'm achieving too. And knowing her secret has never been a burden – in some twisted way it makes me feel powerful, and important. I suppose if this is the closest that I'm going to get to being special, I might as well embrace it.

About year ago I had the great idea of putting together a YouTube showreel to go along with the website I created. I would produce and film it, and all Erica would have to do was make sure that her mask was firmly in place before showing off her stuff.

'Yeah, but then loads of other people, apart from the Vigils, would see it too. I don't know if I want the whole world to see everything yet,' Erica said slowly. She always talks more slowly when she is thinking seriously.

'But everyone is going to see what you can do sooner or later anyway,' I replied.

'Isn't that kinda like saying you might as well eat your

dessert with your main course all together, because it's all going to end up together in your stomach in the end?'

'You want things to happen, don't you? I say we make it happen by ourselves!' I urged.

We must have been talking about it at the same time as those Somerset floods the other year, because I remember that we were watching the footage on YouTube and talking about the Red Rose, a Vigil with a shock of thick fire-engine-red hair (hence the name) and the ability to change the form of anything she touches. Storm tides, under-dredged rivers and some freakishly heavy thunderstorms caused havoc in the South West, and the clip we were watching showed Vigils flipping and flying across the screen like buzzing insects, darting around and into buildings to rescue pets and the elderly from rising waters. The Red Rose spun a celebratory cartwheel in front of the camera after she melted away a particularly precarious fallen tree, the solid wood turning liquid in her hands. Her antics flustered the cameraman, who I presume was perched in a helicopter, as the footage wobbled and struggled to regain focus. Rose is the party Vigil, best friend of speedster Hayley Divine and, like her, always at the latest party or club opening in her trademark skin-tight red outfit, posing and strutting and occasionally showing off with a gymnastic flying move.

'Are you kidding? I wouldn't want to be like the Red Rose,' Erica said at the time, before going to pick out a varnish to paint her nails. 'She's practically naked all the time. I'd be much more sophisticated. And those high heels she wears cannot be comfortable.'

'I'm glad to hear it. You can get all sorts of lower-back problems later on from wearing heels too often,' I said.

'I don't want to be more well-known for the parties I go to than for the good work I do. I mean, don't get me wrong, I will be going to the parties, but they're not everything, you know? Imagine if a tornado hits or something, and I'm all like, "I can't help, I'm afraid. I have a red carpet to walk down!"'

'I don't think you'll be seeing too many tornadoes as a member of the London team.'

'You know what I mean. I know what being a Vigil today is like – it's all a popularity contest. The higher your profile, the better advertising deals you get and the more money you can potentially earn. But sometimes I look back to the glory days, you know, back in the fifties, after the war, when nobody cared about the outfits or how much your arms were insured for. Those were the times when it really meant something to be a superhero. I wish it was still like that. Just because I'm a superhero doesn't mean that I'm cut out to be a celebrity.'

I looked at her. Gleaming waves of golden hair, a perfect figure and bright blue eyes. She was made for everything being a Vigil today means. Maybe her reluctance to be a fully-fledged celebrity as well just added to the perfection.

'I never want people to think I'm as shallow as all that,' Erica said, her voice sad. 'I mean, I know that I'm not brainy or anything, and I can have my shallow moments, but when I look at the Red Rose or Hayley Divine, I can't help but think that they could be so much more.'

'So I guess that's a definite no to the showreel idea?' I said at the time. I can't believe how much our perspectives have changed since then. There was Erica rejecting the video idea, and me pushing her forward. Nowadays it feels like the other way around.

'Let's not even talk about this any more. It's making me think too hard.' She ran her fingers through her hair, shaking it all about. 'Come on, let's do our nails!'

That was the night of the Great Manicure Incident.

'What do you think?' When she was done, Erica held up her freshly manicured fingers, each nail painted a nearly neon pink.

'Beautiful!' I cooed, while finishing off my own lilac paint job.

Erica went back over to my desk and brought up some images on my computer, tapping her fingers carefully on the keyboard so as not to get anything smudged.

'You know much about the Amazing Clara?' she asked me.

'Wasn't she a Vigil back in the sixties?' I offer.

'She was the first official female Vigil,' Erica says. 'I mean, there must have been girls with superpowers before then, but she was the first one who was allowed on the team. And this was back when there was only one Vigil team, in New York. They hadn't even set up the Paris one yet. It was just the Amazing Clara, and all these guys flying around.'

I adjusted myself from my position on my rug to look at the picture on the computer screen properly, hands fanned out in front to stop me from messing up my nails. The Amazing Clara didn't look at all like superheroes today. She looked kind of like a pilot, in jodhpurs, a flying jacket and goggles; there were no corporate-sponsor patches to be seen anywhere. The photo was in black and white, but you still got a sense of the colour of her. The smile indicated rosy cheeks, and her hair was sleek and brunette, coiffed into something probably quite fashionable at the time.

'She's pretty,' I said.

'She was fearless,' said Erica. 'And she didn't care about how pretty she was, or how good she looked. There was this mudslide that obliterated a school in Westchester, just north of New York, and she went right in there and saved all these kids – she could create these air pockets or something that kept everyone alive long enough for them all to be rescued – and then when she emerged she was covered in dirt and mud and was still smiling.'

'That's pretty cool,' I said as Erica showed me the after-rescue pictures.

'I just want you to remind me, in case I ever become incredibly silly to the point of no return, that nobody cared what the Amazing Clara looked like, OK?'

'I'll remember that,' I promised.

'I mean, I can still be girlie, and silly sometimes, but when it comes to the important stuff I want to be just like her.'

She went to lie on my bed, flopping herself tummy down with her arms hanging off the end, still admiring her manicure. She started absently rubbing her fingers together, causing just enough friction to create a whisper of a flame, a slight orange glow like when a candle is just about to go out. I didn't mind her doing this in my room, mostly because I was just pleased to provide her with somewhere that she could play around without fear of being caught or exposed. But then she screamed.

Her fingernails were on fire! The light from her hands had gone, but her actual fingernails were still sizzling. The smell was immediate and awful.

'Oh my God!' Erica yelped. I told her to hush in case my mum heard, and then ran out of the room to dampen a towel that I could wrap around her smouldering hands.

When I got back from the bathroom I discovered that Erica had used my bedsheets to dowse the flames. I had to chuck them out of course, and when my mum asked why, I said it was because I had singed them practising with Erica's hair straighteners.

'But your hair is perfectly straight already!' my mum had exclaimed, after she had stopped ranting about fire risks. Trust me, I already knew all about those.

'Yes, but Erica was showing me how to *curl* my hair with them,' I'd explained, before thanking the heavens that my mum didn't notice at the time that my hair wasn't so much as kinked.

After that episode, my mum banned hair straighteners, and I banned Erica from using her powers in my house. I also haven't been able to even *look* at a bottle of nail varnish again. I like to tell myself that I wear my nails naked now out of solidarity with Erica, who will never wear nail varnish again (she actually mourned this loss, ceremoniously throwing out each colour with a cry of 'Oh why, cruel world? Why!'), but truthfully I've never forgotten that smell. There's something about toxic burning chemicals that scars you for life... my nose is wrinkling now just at the thought of it.

Fortunately I'm quickly distracted from that particular memory by my phone buzzing on my desk. It's a message from Toby.

Whatcha doing? he asks.

Coursework, I text back. It's not as if I can say what I'm really doing: watching old Vigil clips, reminiscing and procrastinating instead of sewing up a supersuit.

There's a delay, and I watch my phone as I wait for him to text again. He doesn't ever just send me a mundane text without it being a preamble to something else. My heart hovers in my chest, resisting the next beat as I wait.

Have you thought any more about the cinema tomorrow? he finally messages.

Honestly, I was trying not to. I had thought, seeing as he hadn't mentioned it again, Toby had forgotten that he'd even asked me. Erica was far too absorbed with her plans with Jay to quiz me on it, and now it was Friday night, and surely if Toby was really keen on seeing me he would have asked during the day? We had the whole of lunchtime together in the library yesterday for him to bring it up.

I know he's not asking me out on a date, because he said that there would be other people there, but even so, just pondering giving him an answer is enough to cause me to physically freeze. I don't think I can get away with a 'maybe', not like in real life. I want to reply. I want to be one of those girls who is effortlessly cool, who can swing her hair over her shoulders and not care what a boy thinks about her, but I'm not. And I blush really, really easily. I'm blushing now, just from thinking of replying to him. How does Erica find this so easy? Arranging her date with Jay seemed so simple. They were going to meet at the cinema, and go for dinner at a fast-food place in the shopping centre opposite. Simple. So why, when Toby isn't even actually asking me out on a proper date, do I find this so hard?

Then I make a decision, one I know that I will want to change straight away, which leaves me just a few seconds to write:

Yes, let's go!

The instant I press send I throw the phone down on my desk as if it's radioactive. I imagine Erica next to me, rubbing my shoulders and congratulating me on my bravery, before giving me a playful thump with her hot fist for being so ludicrous about the whole thing. Except that she's not here. She's spending time with one of her other friends doing some make-up trials or something so that she'll look perfect for her hot date with Jay.

The phone buzzes with a new text message. I know that it's Toby, of course I know that it's Toby, but I can't look at it. I'm too embarrassed. I know that there's no rational reason to be embarrassed, because this isn't a date and any emotional significance I'm giving to this situation is purely in my head, but I am.

Finally, after a few deep breaths, I brace myself:

Cool! I'll meet you at yours at 2!

7

Toby looks so different out of his school uniform, but I guess I do too. He immediately tells me that I look nice, but I think he's just being polite, because I'm wearing a big jumper that I knitted myself last winter, hoping that I might have had a growth spurt by now. My fingers curl up with anxiety under the too-long sleeves. Don't ask me why I decided that this would be the perfect outfit. I must have tried on everything I have before I put this jumper on and left it there. If everything else fails, I'm able to hide myself quite well within it.

I guess he actually looks nice too, but I'm too nervous to even look at him properly, let alone actually say anything about it.

'So, this is cool,' he says when we reach the bus stop.

'Yup,' I reply.

I bounce on my toes. He does the same. I check my watch. So does Toby. Neither of us says anything for a while.

'Uh . . . Just so you know, the others couldn't make it today. There's a Faecraft sale on at the Games Workshop.

But you're cool if it's just the two of us, right?'

'Right! Yeah, sure! No problem!' My voice comes out much louder and more high-pitched than I intended.

This whole thing has become ten times more awkward than I ever thought it could possibly get. My only hope is that Erica and Jay will already be at the cinema when we get there, so that she can save me from dying of cringe. You'd think that if I had a crush on a boy (and, to be honest, I'm still not completely comfortable calling it that), that I'd want to spend as much time with him as possible. It's not like that at all. Every nerve ending in my body is telling me to run away as fast as I can and hide for eternity.

When the bus comes (finally!) Toby gallantly steps back and makes a point of letting me get on first, like he's trying to be a gentleman. When I find a seat he takes the one right next to me, and because we're both wearing jumpers and big coats, he suddenly feels really, really close. I catch myself holding my breath, and I realise that if I turned my head our faces would be just inches apart. We endure the bus ride in total silence.

It's strange because I spend so much time with Toby in school, and we talk so much, and yet this feels so entirely different. Is it me making it different, or is it him? I feel like this isn't the Toby I know, the one with the messy tie and raggedy school blazer, his school trousers coming down past his feet and ending up threadbare at the hems. I know that Toby. That Toby is comfortable and funny and

71

safe. *This* Toby wears Converse sneakers, has fixed his hair with some gel or product or something and looks like a proper boy, a boy that might actually go on dates. I'm hyperaware of the breadth of his shoulders, and the lines on his hands. I have no idea how or why I'm here with him, and that frightens me far more than any fireball Erica could conjure.

Just before we reach the road to the cinema, the bus takes an unexpected turning. Everyone is looking out of the window, and then at each other.

'Sorry about this,' the bus driver announces. 'Seems we've been put on a diversion. Sit tight and we'll get around it.'

By the time we get to the cinema, we're too late for the showing we wanted to see, but it doesn't matter anyway because there's a police cordon around the area and a couple of fire engines are parked up nearby. We can't even get close.

Toby goes to find out what's happening. I scan the crowd for Erica.

'Apparently there's a fire in the industrial yard next door,' Toby tells me when he returns, and sure enough I can now see a faint pillar of black smoke rising up and mingling with the cotton-wool clouds, staining them an ashy grey.

'They're trying to control the blaze,' Toby continues explaining, 'but because there are gas cylinders in one of the outbuildings, they have to evacuate the area, just in case they blow up.'

'Yikes.'

'Yeah, blows, right?'

I try to smile at Toby's lame joke, but I'm too focused on what's going on behind the cinema complex.

More fire engines and other emergency vehicles are on their way; I can hear their sirens wailing in the distance. I'm thinking that there might be something in all of this. That this could be the opportunity Erica's been waiting for. It's then that I spot her heading towards the cinema from the other direction, on her own, looking down at her phone with an anxious expression. I wonder where Jay is, and guess from the look on her face that Erica is thinking the same.

This might be one of those moments where you can see your life splitting in two and going down very different paths. In one world I go over to Erica and tell her that it's finally time for her to save the day. I tell her to dash to mine to get the costume, before flying back and helping the fire crews with the imminent disaster. In the other world I stay right here with Toby as the professionals do their thing, and then Jay turns up and he and Erica move their date elsewhere. Flamegirl doesn't save the day and everything continues exactly as it has been, with Erica remaining frustrated and me content as life goes on unchanged.

But even as I'm thinking about the possibilities, I find that I'm wandering away from Toby and over towards Erica.

'Hey,' I say.

'Lou!' Erica cries, throwing her arms around me. 'I've been wandering around for twenty minutes already, and Jay isn't even here. He couldn't have stood me up, could he? Please tell me he hasn't stood me up!'

'I'm sure he's just stuck on the buses. They're all on diversion,' I explain.

'But he rides a motorbike,' Erica reminds me.

'Traffic, then?' I shrug.

'What's going on anyway? Why aren't they letting people into the cinema?'

'Erica...' I pause, giving myself one last chance to back out. But I can't. 'Here are my house keys. You need to go back and get into costume, quickly. This could be your chance!'

'What are you talking about? How?'

'There's a fire in those warehouses behind the cinema. And there are gas cylinders in there. If the fire spreads and they overheat, they could blow up. We learned about this in chemistry, remember? You could get them out of there.'

'And then what?' she asks, already panicked.

'I don't know – try and fly them away somewhere safe? Allow them to cool down far away from the fire?'

'Right. Yes. OK, I can do that.'

'This is your chance. It's daylight, and the police are here and everything.'

We look at each other, and for a moment I think she's going to cry. Then she dashes away in the direction of home, and I wonder if I've done the right thing, because I've not seen Erica look that scared in a long time, and what if this all goes horribly wrong? I glimpse that other, parallel world, where I didn't say or do anything. But I'd never forgive myself if I'd known there was an opportunity for Erica and we'd missed it. It would feel like a betrayal. This is my job after all; it's why Erica needs me.

'What's happening?' Toby asks, coming right up next to me. 'Want to see if they open up the cinema again – they might start the film a bit later – or go get something to eat?'

Now that I know Flamegirl is going to be making an appearance, Toby doesn't seem to matter nearly so much. All that anxiety vanished as soon as I went into Sensible Mode.

I suggest that we grab some greasy food from the chicken place across the road, just for something to do. I don't know how long Erica is going to be. I'm thinking about how lucky it is that I finished patching up the suit this morning, but then I'm also wondering how on earth she's going to get the zip at the back all the way up without my help. It's possible, just awkward. We get some chicken strips and fries in brown paper bags that go see-through from the grease, and a couple of giant cups of Coke. I have to manoeuvre carefully to make sure I pay for myself – I just know that Toby is going to offer and then it will all just get far too weird. So I order and pay for my food straight away, leaving Toby to fend for himself.

Maybe I'm imagining it, but when we emerge from the restaurant there's a certain static in the air, a buzz of something unfamiliar. Butterflies crowd in my belly as I notice a helicopter patrolling high above us, and now there are extra police and firemen milling around the cordoned-off zone. I hear the most senior-looking officers muttering the phrases 'large-scale evacuation' and 'highly flammable'. I think of those gas cylinders, hot and volatile, and hope that Erica remembers enough from her chemistry revision to be able to sort it all out safely.

There's an urgent crackle from the nearest police officer's radio, and suddenly everyone is looking up to the sky. Only I know what we're all waiting for.

She appears like a burst of sunbeam through a low cloud. It's thrilling. Bystanders are gasping and pointing and it's like the rest of the world has stopped moving. I want to know what she's thinking, what she can see, and whether she needs help with a plan. Except that I can't have anything more to do with this situation. We can't risk anyone finding out our true identities. I have to pretend to be just another random bystander.

Flamegirl lands right next to the small conference of police and firemen. She stands strong, hands on hips and face fierce under that black mask, as she asks what the problem is and how she can help. I'm slightly too far away to hear what they say in reply.

Next thing I know, Flamegirl is flying high above the cinema. I watch as she dives down towards the roof of the warehouse building, but I can't see much more because of all the smoke. Then she's back, flying up again, and her arms are clasped around a heavy-looking canister. She climbs higher and higher, until she's nothing more than a distant speck against the clouds. I presume she's looking for somewhere safe to set the cylinder down.

And then, the explosion.

It's a massive fireball of red and orange with thick black smoke rising out in ugly tendrils. We shield our eyes and cower from any potential debris that may be falling, and by the time we all turn back to the sky, Flamegirl has gone.

My heart feels as if it's going to beat its way right out of my chest. Did she mean to do that? Is she OK? Or did her nervous, overheated hands cause the explosion accidentally? Did she blow herself up? I'm panicking now. This is all too much for her – I've pushed her into something deadly before she can handle it. If she's been hurt, it'll be all my fault.

But as the smoke begins to clear, we see her again, hovering high above us, her hair trailing golden like it might be made of flame too. She waits for a moment (regaining her composure?) before she takes a quick dive back down to the warehouse building.

She retrieves another cylinder, flies it up as high as before, and once again it explodes. Explosion after explosion rocks the sky until the spectators don't even scream any more. We watch in awe, as if some grand fireworks display is happening just for us, each blast joining to form a great tentacled octopus of smoke high above. After each boom I wait until I see her fly back downwards before I let myself breathe out. I regret not finding a way to test this side of her powers further. How much explosive heat can she handle? What is *too much*? And then, a thought that gives me a chill as it sneaks into my brain: what if there's no explosion that she *can't* endure?

Finally, apparently content that the site is clear and safe, she jets out and over us, landing back next to the group of police and firemen.

I presume that she's checking in with them, making sure the job's been done and that she's good to go. At first I wonder why she isn't rushing over to me, why she's not even looking in my direction, and then I remember: she can't. I'll admit it hurts a little bit, if only because I feel like I'm involved too – I am the one that sewed her costume and told her what to do after all – but the rational side of my brain reassures me that Flamegirl needs this moment alone. For the safety of our true identities, she can't be seen with me right now. I send her a text, telling her I'll meet her back at my house, and I smile when I see her reaching for the newly sewn zip pocket on her upper arm and checking her phone.

Then I remember Toby. He's still standing just behind me, his fast food discarded at his feet, and most of his Coke fizzing in puddles on the pavement.

'That. Was. Awesome!' he says. 'I mean, you did see that, right? A Vigil! Here! In our own town! The guys won't believe that they missed this!'

'You're OK if we head back home now, right?' I ask him. 'I mean, who knows if the cinema is going to open up again this afternoon, and that was all very exciting and everything—'

'No worries, no worries. I think I'm going to go to the Games Workshop anyway. You know, to tell the guys!'

'No problem.'

We're standing a good metre apart, and I can see that Toby's desperate to go and share the news about a new superhero on the beat. I, meanwhile, am bursting to get back to my place to check that Erica's OK, but it seems strange just abandoning Toby here. Neither of us knows how to say goodbye – handshake? hug? – but in the end I give him this stupid little wave (my hand completely enveloped by my jumper sleeve) and turn and dart for the bus stop.

'Going viral' is a phrase I thought I understood. But I never imagined what it would actually be like to be stuck in the middle of a virtual whirlwind.

All I can do is listen, and seem politely interested whenever anyone brings up the subject of Flamegirl. Which is pretty much all the time. All Monday morning my teachers have been struggling to keep the class under control as rumours and gossip fly between the students. The excitement ripples as kids turn to chat and show each other the latest pictures and news on their phones.

'How are you not more excited by all of this?' Toby demands at lunchtime. He demands it rather quietly, because we're sitting opposite each other in the library trying to get on with some extra maths work.

Toby has more reason than most to be extra-excited by everything Flamegirl. He was there. He's like a celebrity by proxy. Year Sevens have been following him in the corridors all morning, daring each other to go up and speak to him, and suddenly he's got dozens of friend requests on Facebook.

'It's another superhero. So what?' I don't even have to act my disinterest by this point. A whole morning of catching everybody else's conversations and listening to Toby go on about who from the popular crowd has 'added' him has been enough to tire me out.

'But this isn't *just another* superhero. This is one that belongs to us! And, need I emphasise just how absolutely amazing she is?'

'Maybe I'm just not as interested in the whole super-hero thing as everybody else,' I suggest.

Toby's staring at me.

'What?' I whisper-shout.

'Seriously? You're seriously trying to tell me that even though you were right there, standing next to me when it all happened, when we saw someone flying right before our eyes, that you're *just not as interested* as everybody else? Did you not *see* her? Did you not hear those explosions?'

'Toby, she's just a person.'

'A person who can fly! Who we might have walked past one day on the high street!'

'But still a person. Who we don't know.'

He mutters something I can't make out and then goes back to his maths equations. I watch him for a while, trying to think of something I could say that would bring his attention favourably back to me. I wonder what it would be like if I told him the truth, that I'm secretly the master-mind behind the whole thing. Would he think that I'm as awesome as he obviously thinks she is? Would he think about me in the same way he just gazed into space, thinking about her?

Erica was horribly sick when she finally got back to my house on Saturday. I was there before her, as she had to hang around and talk to the emergency services, as well as do some interviews with a couple of local journalists who were there to cover the fire. After she climbed through my window, I helped her to the bathroom and combed her hair away from her face with my fingers as she puked.

'Are you OK?' I asked. She'd never reacted this way to anything we'd ever done in practice.

'No,' Erica slurred. 'I'm dying.'

'Really?'

'Probably not.' She laid herself down on the cool bathroom tiles of my floor. 'What's happening to me?'

'Did you do anything different? Have you ever felt sick before and not told me?'

'No. But then I've never flown as fast as that, or as high as that. And I've never been in the middle of an explosion either. And everyone had their phones out filming me. Did you see that? Everyone!'

'Well, it could be G-force. Possibly.'

'What's that?'

'Well, basically it kind of means you might have squished your brain a little bit when you flew, because you were going so fast. Like when you're on a roller coaster.'

'I hate roller coasters.' She moaned again and then rolled over so that I couldn't see her face.

'Or it could be all the excitement. Or maybe nerves.'

'I can't go having a freaking panic attack every time I save the world! What kind of stupid superhero would I be then?'

'Well, let's just hope that this is a one-off then. Probably is. This was the first time, after all. It was bound to be a bit scary. And answering questions about it all straight away couldn't have been easy.' Sometimes I wonder if I can possibly sound too sensible. 'Maybe you should stay here tonight so that I can watch you? You know, in case it's a G-force concussion-type thing?'

'One of those journalist people said something about arson. How messed up is that? When I was talking to them afterwards – that's why it took me so long getting back here by the way – they said that the lockups should have been empty on a Saturday and wanted to know if I'd seen anything suspicious. Don't you think that's strange?'

'Never mind that – what was with all those explosions anyway? I thought you were going to move the cylinders to a safe place to cool down?'

'I thought that too. But it turns out that I couldn't keep my hands cool enough. Ugh, when that first boom happened? That was horrible. I thought I had ruined everything. I thought that everyone was going to think that I couldn't handle one simple job. Once I had gone in and got the first cylinder out, I could feel it hissing and shaking, and then it seemed that the only thing I could do was let it explode, but only after I'd got it to a safe height. Sure turned out to be a good show, right?'

'It's not about the show, remember. What would the Amazing Clara have done in the same circumstances?' I tried not to make it sound like a scold, but apparently failed miserably.

'The Amazing Clara didn't have hands that were on fire,' Erica snapped before quickly changing the subject. 'Did I ruin your date?'

'It wasn't a date.'

Even though I couldn't see her face properly, I knew that she was smiling, still trying to tease me despite her pain. 'Well, mine didn't even get started. Jay never turned up. And I swear that I saw his motorbike parked around the corner, but then I suppose all bikes look the same. I looked for him afterwards as well, in case he saw Flamegirl but not me. But nothing. He never showed. Stood up! How depressing is that?'

'I think you should be thinking about resting up and not about a boy you hardly even know.'

'You are such a spoilsport!' she teased. 'But that's one of the reasons I love you. And thanks for giving me the push earlier. I don't know what I'd do without you. You know that, right?'

I helped Erica up off the floor and out of the costume, which was singed and shredded all over the place. Definitely not rescuable, which was a shame. Erica told me that a paramedic handed her one of those silver emergency blankets to wrap around herself for all the photos, and I can imagine her wearing it like a bright metallic cape. Starting from scratch on the costume is going to be a nightmare, especially if we're going to have to chuck them away every time Flamegirl makes an appearance. I'd have to research more suitable materials.

I let Erica rest on my bed while I went downstairs to have dinner with my family, like nothing unusual was going on. When I went back up to my room, Erica was gone. I went online to order another costume, and mumbled in frustration when I realised that, because of Halloween, it would take longer to arrive.

I didn't hear from Erica for the rest of the weekend. She didn't reply to any of my texts.

I've been hoping to talk to Erica all day, if only to find out if she's all right. The few times we've passed each other today, there's been nothing. Sure, she smiles at me, and I got a cheerful wave in French, but there is something forced and fake about it too, something that makes me worry why she didn't get in touch all of Sunday. What I really want is a serious word about what we're going to do next. Rationally I know that we're both behaving exactly as we usually do in school, but right now that doesn't feel like enough. I look over to the terrace outside the library, and there she is, her skin fresh and her hair all shiny in its bouncy ponytail. She gossips and laughs with her friends and is obviously pretending to be just as amazed and fascinated by Flamegirl as anybody else. But even from here I can tell that something isn't right. She has the same look that my mum gets when she has a migraine but doesn't want to worry anyone with it. I'm desperate to know what she's thinking. Have I done something wrong?

'Hey! Look at this!' Toby exclaims suddenly, as loudly as it's possible to exclaim in a library being monitored by the tireless Mrs Fraser.

'What?'

'Can you believe that Flamegirl already has a fan-art site? And someone's done these manga mock-ups and they're basically just awesome! I might have to get a print or something.'

'Are you kidding me?'

'Want to look?'

I nod in reply and Toby sneaks his phone to me under the table. I hold it down in my lap so that Mrs Fraser can't see. Sure enough, there's a whole Japanese-style art site dedicated to Flamegirl, black-catsuited, masked and yellow-haired, all exaggerated hips and sexy poses. Some of the pictures are a bit obscene actually, so I pass the phone back to Toby as quickly as I can, disgusted.

'That is awful.'

'I thought that you weren't interested in Flamegirl anyway. I thought she was "just a person",' Toby tuts at me.

'I'm not. She is.'

'So then why were you so eager to look at Flamegirl manga?' And even though I know he's teasing me, I find myself responding anyway.

'What is this – some kind of weird trick? I can't believe how quickly that stuff appears on the internet. It's only been a couple of days! Plus it's so disgusting. You never see the guy superheroes posing with their bums and chests sticking out. It's just sexist.'

'You know what I think? I think you're trying to seem all cool and "above" the superhero thing. But really you're just as obsessed as everybody else. I see right through you, Louise Kirby.'

Toby stares straight at me, his eyes grey and gleaming. I dare myself to hold his gaze as long as possible, just so that I can keep looking at him looking at me like that, but as my heart rate quickens, I find myself blushing.

'I'm not obsessed,' I huff.

Even though it's not the end of lunch yet I start to pack up my stuff to leave. Being so close to Toby while he's teasing me like this is becoming annoying. I'm apparently failing abysmally at controlling my hormonal responses.

This won't do at all.

'Where are you going?' he asks.

'I don't need to hear all of this.' I make to leave, acutely aware that Toby is also packing up his things and rushing to catch up with me.

'Come on, Louise, admit it! You're a sucker for the supers, just the same as the rest of us!' he calls as he catches up with me. I daren't turn to look at him because of all the blushing.

'No, I'm not.'

'What is it? A crush on Quantum? Or is Deep Blue more your style?' He's practically chasing me down the corridor now.

'I don't care about superheroes.'

'Yes, you do!'

I stop, turn and brace myself in front of him, holding onto the straps of my backpack for strength. 'I don't give a crap about superheroes! And I especially don't give a crap about stupid Flamegirl!' I practically yell, and I'm pretty sure that if I was actually Flamegirl I'd have fireballs shooting out from my eyes right now.

'Hi, Louise.' I turn back round, and Erica is right there. Right. There.

'Hi, Erica,' I mumble.

I hope I'm imagining it, but she looks hurt.

'Um... are we still on for tonight?' Erica asks me, biting at her bottom lip.

I'm telling her with my eyes that I'm only trying to stop Toby harassing me and that this is just me doing the whole secret-identity thing as best I can, but I doubt she's understanding this.

'Of course! I'll see you later?'

'Yep, see you later.' She's trying to sound all bright and breezy as she wanders off with her friends.

'I was only teasing, you know?' Toby says, coming up close to me and faux-punching my shoulder.

I feel the blush creep back up my neck and decide that the only way out of this is to just brush the whole thing off like it never happened.

'Of course. I know that.'

'We OK?'

I want to tell him that as long as he doesn't start swooning over Flamegirl right in front of me we're going to be fine. But because I don't know how to explain why his swooning hurts me, all I say is, 'Sure.'

She's trying to pretend that things aren't weird, but they definitely are. I can tell this because she's actually getting on with her homework, not trying to get me talking about inane school gossip. She's quiet and appears studious, but she is checking her phone every other minute. Maybe she's checking the time to see when she can get away from me. I hate being paranoid, but Erica's making it far too easy.

'Are you feeling better now? No more sickness?' I ask, but I have to say the first bit again because I'm mumbling so much.

'Yep.'

'No headaches or dizzy spells or anything?'

'Nope.'

'Have you ever thought about how your physiology might be different to regular people's?'

'Not really.' At least that was three syllables.

She doesn't even look at me, and the thought that she might be genuinely pissed off makes my stomach twist. And I don't know what to say to make it better. Erica's staring at the page of her textbook, but I doubt she's actually reading. She's twirling a pen in her fingers, and I watch silently as the heat from her hands melts the plastic and the shell of the biro splits in two and falls away.

'I need to borrow a pen.' Erica's voice is flat as she tucks away the molten remnants into her pencil case. From the way she sits up suddenly, I think she is going to say something else, but she just starts biting at her bottom lip again.

'I don't want you to melt it.'

'Fine. I'll go home then.'

'No, don't go. I'll get you another pen.'

I give her one of my smarter ones, to show her that I don't care if she accidentally destroys it. She could turn my curtains into twin pillars of flame right now if she wanted to, I'm so desperate for her to be OK.

'Please talk to me, Erica,' I mumble.

She just continues to blank-stare at the textbook, until I get uncomfortable and return to my biology notes.

'Today has totally sucked,' she sighs unexpectedly.

I bookmark my page. 'Why?' I'm cautious. I don't want to scare her off.

'Do you have any idea what I've had to cope with today?'

'You seemed fine when I saw you around—'

'It's all this pretending. And not being able to talk to anyone. And when I saw you at lunch I was actually coming to find you so that I could tell you why I blanked you on Sunday, and I needed to get away from the girls because they were driving me absolutely crazy. I thought I was going to cry because they're convinced that Flame-girl must be a slut or something. But then I hear you mouthing off about me too. That's why I'm angry, OK? I know you've been pretending as well, but it isn't the same for you. It can't be the same.'

'I didn't realise. I mean, I thought . . . but I didn't actually realise.'

'They were saying horrible things about my hair, and my arms, and how fat I am.'

'You're not fat.'

'Whatever. It's been wearing me down all day. I didn't think it was going to be like this, that people would say things like that.'

'You did an awesome job on Saturday. Imagine if those cylinders had actually exploded right where they were! It could have been terrible. You're a proper superhero now. This is what you wanted,' I remind her. 'And I'm sorry that you heard me shouting like that at lunch. You know it wasn't actually about you, right?'

'Yeah, I know. I've had a rough day. And there are lots of feelings happening right now.'

'You know that Toby is in love with you, right? I mean, not with *you* you, but with Flamegirl. It kind of got to me. That's why I was so worked up and why I shouted.'

'He'll get over it.' Erica smiles, before pausing and looking down. 'There's something else . . .'

'What?'

She takes a long pause and recrosses her legs, apparently getting comfortable while also stalling for time. She looks down at the floor, not at me, and lets her hair hang in a blonde wave in front of her face.

'Another reason I'm all angsty and stuff – it's what I wanted to talk to you about at lunch, but I didn't know how you'd take it. I don't know how you'll take it now in fact . . . It's about why I didn't speak to you on Sunday.'

'What is it?' She's making me nervous.

'It's Jay.'

'Did you find out why he stood you up?'

'He didn't stand me up.'

'So, what, then?'

'Louise...Jay's one of them. Jay's a Vigil. They've found me.'

It turns out that it was his motorbike that Erica saw outside the park last week. And here it is again, propped up in the same place right now. I don't know why I agreed to this, and here, of all places, except that I couldn't come up with any way to get out of it. This has all become very real, and I feel as if I'm desperately trying to cling on to something that is speeding away from me as fast as it can go.

What bugs me the most is that Jay didn't want me to know. The reason Erica was so distant on Sunday, and so fraught about telling me on Monday evening, was that he asked her not to say anything. But she couldn't, she had to tell me, and I suppose I should feel happy and relieved about that. But she still kept the truth from me for nearly two days, and contemplated not telling me at all, because of a stranger. A stranger who comes with no credentials other than his word, and who pretty much stalked us for a month, as far as I can work out. Possibly even longer. What would have happened if Erica hadn't revealed who Jay really was? Would she suddenly have disappeared, only to emerge again on the Vigil A-team without telling me? Part of me is furious with her for this parallel timeline that hasn't even happened, while another part is furious with the Vigils for even trying to make it happen. But the biggest part of me is furious with Jay himself, for trying to steal Erica away.

'He doesn't know you're coming, OK? So be cool,' Erica says as we walk across the field.

Apparently Jay is waiting for us at the tunnel. Don't even get me started on how angry I am about that. The tunnel is *our* place, and *him* being there just pollutes it. This sneaky infiltration into our lives makes me suspicious. My fists clench up inside my sleeves. I wonder if I have it in me to punch him, because right now that's exactly what I'd like to do.

As if he's actually trying to make the situation worse, he's smoking as he leans against the curved wall of the tunnel. He's quite obviously seen us approaching, but he's chosen to stay all aloof, gazing into space and blatantly trying to look cool and dangerous. I will concede that he's a typically good-looking guy, but there's a darkness to him that's a complete turn-off. He looks up at us through his dark, floppy hair, squinting and frowning, and I wonder if he's trying to be all intense and thoughtful or just needs to go and have his eyesight checked. He's skinny, like he doesn't eat enough, pale like he stays up all night and sleeps all day, and is enveloped in this giant black trench coat, the kind that would billow out around him as he walked. It's not that I don't understand what all the girls see in him – I'm not oblivious – but I don't think it's authentic.

'Please don't be all pissy,' Erica pleads as we get closer. But actually I think it's him she needs to say it to.

'What's she doing here?' he asks as soon as we're within earshot.

'I had to tell her, OK?' Erica says. She doesn't sound quite as determined as I'd like her to.

I fold my arms across my chest. He throws down his cigarette and stamps it out with his foot.

'I thought I explained to you how this works. No unknown variables,' he sneers, talking to Erica but looking at me.

'Louise is a part of this. I can't do it without her.'

'That's not how this works.'

I think Erica's too nervous – or too enthralled – to argue back. But she stands close to me, and there's an uncomfortable silence as Jay considers his options. I'm here, and I know what's going on. He can't take that away. He also can't make me leave. He's not a teacher with a detention slip, he's just a guy, and this is a public place. And yet my heart is hammering, and all the adrenaline is confusing. Do I want to fight him, or do I want to run away?

'So, Jay, this is Louise. And Louise, this is Jay.' I don't think I've ever seen Erica look or sound so awkward.

He just stares at me, unsure where to go next and daring me to make a move.

'So, Erica says you're a Vigil,' I start. I try my hardest not to stammer it, but I'm sure that I sound pretty pathetic anyway. Confrontations are definitely not my forte. Besides which, I'm now wondering if he has any superpowers of his own. What if he could vaporise me on the spot? He considers me before replying. I wonder about his true age. Now that I'm really looking at him, I can't imagine that he's younger than twenty. How was he even allowed in our school? Was it all just a ruse to seek Erica out?

'I work for them, yes,' he finally replies.

'So what's going on exactly? What is all this?'

'I'm a recruiter. I came for Erica.'

'How did you find us?'

He chuckles to himself, rolling his eyes at what he obviously considers a stupid question. Except that I don't think that it is a stupid question. I think it's important, and scary.

'You must know that I can't tell you about that.' He pauses, considering again. 'All you need to know is that we found you. I gathered intel, I made my reports, and the decision is to bring Erica in for more tests. It's a process. And Erica is still young, so things might take some time. But in short, as I've already told Erica, we're interested. The Vigils are interested.'

'And you expect me to just go away now?'

'Louise!' Erica starts, amazed at what I can only describe as my 'balls'. The truth is, I'm pumped up with fury and anxiety and somehow it's making me far more confrontational than I've ever been before.

Jay sighs. 'That was the original plan.'

'Louise is a part of this,' Erica says. 'She stays with me, or else you don't have me.'

'I can appreciate that that's what you're saying, yes. Except that my bosses won't be too happy with it.'

'What were you going to do? Whisk Erica away and pretend that I don't exist?'

Jay squints at me again, still frowning, and then he turns and bends down towards his bag. I look at Erica, who shrugs. Jay retrieves some plain pieces of paper and goes to sit down on the bench.

'You'll have to sign some forms,' he says.

'What kind of forms?' I ask, peering over at the white pages. They're blank.

'Confidentiality forms. They're from Vigil HQ and are government approved. You sign them, we keep them. Understand?'

'OK, but where are they exactly?'

Jay looks up at me from behind that ridiculous mess of brown hair and sighs again, obviously aggravated. I try not to care. Then he lays out a single sheet on one knee and proceeds to place both of his hands over it. There's barely a sound, just a slight crackling in the air, and nobody has moved, but something has happened. I look towards Erica, confused, before turning back to Jay, who presents me with the sheet of paper, now covered in small and complicated-looking words.

'How did you...?' I start.

'Jay has a superpower too,' Erica finishes.

'Is this another thing you're not meant to tell me about?' I ask her.

'I have a photographic memory and can convey the images I see in my head to paper or fabric or stuff like that, by way of an ink my hands produce,' Jay explains.

'So you're a human photocopier?' I say.

He peers up, chewing his bottom lip. I feel as if I've hit a particularly painful nerve, because when he looks back up at me he's sneering, like he wants to say something terrible to me.

'Don't call me that,' he grumbles, biting his tongue.

'But your Vigil codename is Copyboy, right?' Erica asks.

'That's the name they gave me. Doesn't mean I like it.'

I look down at the piece of paper, which is now a legitimate confidentiality contract, and remember that my dad once told me to always read something thoroughly before signing it. I fold up the paper and put it in my bag, explaining to Jay that I'll read it properly when I get home. He looks furious.

'So I guess you've seen Erica on the internet,' I say, more because we're all so uncomfortable around each other than because I actually want to chat. But I presume that's why Jay has revealed himself now, and not before.

'Something like that,' Jay replies.

'There's something else I haven't told you,' Erica mutters. 'But promise you won't get angry, OK?'

I stare at Erica, wondering what on earth could possibly make me more annoyed than I am now, but she pauses, apparently unsure of what to say next. So Jay decides to say it instead.

'The thing at the weekend, it was all a test. We needed to see what Erica could do. And she passed, so now here we are.'

'A test?' The truth doesn't hit home at first. Then I realise: the fire was staged. Did Jay really commit arson just to draw Erica out?

'They needed to see how I would cope under pressure,' Erica tells me. 'Jay knew about my powers, but he had to know how far they went, and what I could do in a crisis.'

'People could have been hurt!' I cry. There it is. The feelings are hitting me, loud and angry and appalled.

'Nobody was hurt,' Jay sighs, clearly bored of this. He rubs at his eyes like he's trying to wipe away my presence.

'That's not the point!' Why isn't Erica more furious? 'But they could have been! What if your arson plan had gone wrong? Or what if Erica couldn't sort everything out? Or worse, what if she got hurt?'

'There's no point dwelling on this now,' Jay yawns.

'It's fine, Louise, it's really fine,' Erica tries to calm me.

'How can you say that? Is this what the Vigils do? Is this how they behave?'

'I'm given my task, and I get it done the best way I know how,' Jay explains. 'Sometimes things have got to go a bit wrong for them to eventually go a lot right. Sometimes a bit of calamity is what it takes to make the good stuff happen.'

'That's how you're justifying *arson*? The means don't matter, only the end?' I just can't believe that is right. I'm thinking about Erica, and how nervous she was, and then the panic and the fear of the passers-by and the involvement of the emergency services. And finally I'm thinking about my costume and all the months of work that went into it, completely ruined.

'I had a job to do, and I got it done,' Jay reiterates.

'It's OK, Louise, it really is. I was worried and scared at first. But Jay only did it because he knew I could handle it. He wouldn't have put me in any actual danger, not really, but he had to know what I could do.'

'Erica, that just doesn't seem right. People could have got hurt. And all the damage that was done? Aren't the police investigating?'

'It'll all be sorted out,' Jay says cryptically.

'I just can't believe that the Vigils would endorse this,' I sigh.

'It's done. Get over it.' Jay's tone is final, and it scares me. Who is this guy?

'How do we even know that you're really one of them?' I ask. I wonder if Erica has even thought about this, or whether she's been too starstruck and smitten to care.

'On Thursday, Erica's coming down to the base in London. She'll have a chance to check out the operation, meet some of the team, and then we'll decide where to go from there.'

'Lou, this is what I've always wanted,' Erica says, coming right up to me and holding on to my arm. 'It's actually happening.'

'I think I should come too.'

Jay almost bursts out laughing. 'That would be impossible.'

'Jay, maybe Lou *should* come? She's a part of this, and it wouldn't be right without her.'

'Are you kidding me? They'd never let her anywhere near the building.'

'Well then, I won't be going near the building either.'

I look up at Erica, being bold and standing her ground. For the first time this afternoon I feel like we're actually a team.

'Please be kidding me right now,' Jay groans, clicking out his fingers. I shudder at the noise.

'Come on. She'll have signed the confidentiality thing by then. Surely it wouldn't be all that difficult to get her in.'

'She's not even meant to know about this!' He practically yells it.

'Well, she does. And if you don't have Louise, you don't have me.'

Erica's hand is still clutching my arm. She's getting stressed and overheated. Her grip, although light, is already starting to burn.

'You need to calm down,' I mumble to her, but not softly enough, because Jay still hears.

'You see, this is exactly the kind of thing that my people will be able to help you with. They'll train you so that you'll have complete control over your powers, and will push you to see exactly how far you can go. You do realise that you've not even begun to explore your own potential, right? Only the Vigils will be able to help you to do that.'

'We've been doing a pretty good job so far,' I say.

'You're just a couple of kids,' Jay practically spits.

Erica lets go of my arm and starts to pace, trying to burn off the energy inside her without resorting to conjuring a flame. I can see that she's trying to prove that she has her powers under control, that she won't literally flare up every time that she's annoyed or aggravated. She looks up at me, watching me in a way that makes me think she's seriously considering travelling to London with this freak, alone.

'You shouldn't be alone with him. If you're going to London, then I have to go with you.'

Jay throws his hands up in the air as he stands up. He starts talking to Erica quietly and seriously. I can't believe that he's actually trying to steal Erica away from me, right in front of my eyes.

I look down at my own hands, willing them with all my might to make a fireball. If only I could do something, anything, to be necessary. Just being involved doesn't feel like enough right now, and I wish that I could offer something more than friendship. But I know that Erica needs me. We've been in this together since the beginning, and I'm not prepared to give up on that now.

When I look back up, I notice Jay walking away across the field, his black trench coat billowing behind him like an unnecessarily dramatic cape.

'Where is he going?' I ask.

'Home. He needs to pack up his stuff. He doesn't have to be undercover in our school any more, so he's got to move back to London. I can't believe how angry he is,' Erica says.

'He has no right to be angry. He's the one that's messing everything up!'

'It's OK, Lou-Lou. I think he gets it. He's going to talk to his boss and try to get you in. We'll go down to London, and we'll check this whole thing out, and everything will turn out fine, I promise.'

'You can't promise things like that right now,' I warn her.

'Maybe not, but I can promise you that this is the right thing. We always meant for the Vigils to find me, and now they have. Do I like the way they've done it? No. But we can't change that. It's happened. But maybe we can change the way it happens in the future for other people. I don't know. But this is what we wanted. This is what *I* want.'

'Why does it have to be Jay though? I can't stand him.'

'Lay off him a bit. He's got his job to do, and he thought it was going to be a hell of a lot easier.'

'You still fancy him, don't you? Even after the whole arson thing?'

Erica looks away from me, guilty. 'He's not the guy I thought he was. And he's a bit older, but there's still something... I don't know.'

'It's not a good idea,' I warn her. 'Jay means trouble.'

She sighs, and still can't look me in the eye.

'And besides, what if his stupid fingers get all inky on you?' That she laughs at. 'Does it even wash off?'

'It'll be fine,' she says with finality as we set off back across the field. 'I'm sure of it.'

10

We're wandering along the street right outside the main building of King's College, wondering if we're in the right place. Jay gave Erica very specific instructions about where to be and at what time, but now we're here, and he's nowhere in sight. Erica is pouting, hands clasped around an iced coffee drink, and I'm just gazing at all the buses and the taxis rumbling by, trying not to think too much. The anticipation feels heavy in my stomach, like I'm on a crest of some theme-park ride and about to go over the edge. Except that there aren't any safety harnesses and I don't know how steep the drop is.

I've been into the city on school trips, and a couple of times with my family to go out to eat or to the theatre, but this is the first time I've ever been alone here. Everything seems so vast and energetic. Everyone else appears to be in some great rush, which makes me nervous. Everyone is taller than me, better dressed than me. I feel so small and insignificant.

'Where is he?' Erica huffs, peering down the street one way and then another, but it's hard to make out anything among the crowds of students heading to or from the King's university building, or the business people in their dark coats and frowns. Buses are continually blocking our view of the other side of the street, and my height means that I'm not ideally suited to looking out for brooding Vigil scouts. I lean back against the wall of the building, finding a patch of blue sky above to stare into, and pray that our cover story will hold up.

This is the first time in my life that I've bunked off school. Perhaps Jay purposely chose a school day for this visit because he thought I wouldn't have the nerve to skive off. Not just a school day, but a library day. Without me there as a buffer, there's every chance that Toby will get himself seriously scolded, or worse, fired. But this is ten times more important than library time with Toby, and definitely worth a few white lies. I texted him this morning to let him know that I was ill and probably contagious, and faked illness to my parents too. Weirdly, my mum was thrilled that I was taking the day off – she thinks I work too hard and put too much pressure on myself, and seeing as I've rarely taken a sick day throughout my entire time at secondary school, she was more than happy about calling the school for me. Both my parents work, so as soon as they left the house I snuck out. My only challenge will be getting back home before they do.

I know when Jay arrives just from looking at Erica's face. She's blushing right up to her ears. It's obvious that she still likes him, despite me telling her in my most sensible voice that he's definitely too old for her. Nevertheless, she flicks her hair back and away from her face and smiles so bright and wide that the corners of her eyes completely crease up. I wonder if he realises the effect he has on her, or if he even thinks of himself as leading her on. As far as I can tell, he hasn't tried to put her off. Either he's pathetically ignorant, or I have yet another reason not to trust him.

Right now he doesn't look happy. In fact, he's in Full-On Scowl Mode.

'What are you doing here?' He's looking at me, and his voice is low, and somehow this is far more frightening than being yelled at.

'You know that Louise is a part of this,' Erica says, and even though I'm proud of her for defending me, I'm a little hurt that she hasn't already got permission for me to be here. I thought she was going to talk to Jay about me? I thought everything was going to be *fine*.

'Louise can't be here. You don't understand how sensitive these things are. We can't have just anybody waltzing into this place!'

'I'm not just anybody,' I say. I want to sound proud and brave, but I fear I sound just like the mouse I feel I look like.

'I didn't mean . . .' Jay sighs and runs his hands through his hair. He looks like he wants to scream. 'Look, the others won't be happy about this.'

'What am I meant to do? Hang about on the streets and wait for you to finish up?' I ask.

'We're not leaving Louise out in London on her own,' says Erica. 'I don't see what's wrong with her being here. She's been there for everything else. Besides, I insisted that she come with me, so it's not her fault. Let your bosses shout at me, OK?'

Jay makes some sort of frustrated grunting noise, then says, 'Fine. Have you at least got the confidentiality agreement I gave you? Have you signed it?'

I reach into my backpack and hand him the signed contract. I'm hoping that he'll be impressed that I've put it in a plastic file wallet, sandwiched between two blank sheets of paper so that nobody could tell what it was if it fell out of my bag. Jay doesn't seem to care.

He turns round and leads us just a few hundred metres to a narrow building, the first two storeys clad in shiny maroon brick, the levels above looking just like all the other buildings around here, beige and ancient. The entrance is barred, but a clear sign in the brickwork above says 'Strand Station'. Jay takes a simple key out of the pocket of his trench coat, unlocks a door in the grille of the barrier and gestures for us to follow him inside.

It's an old London Underground ticket office, dark because the semicircular window above the doorway is coated in grime, and every surface is covered in dust. Not the fine kind of dust you get at home, but proper grey balls of fluff that roll across the tiled floor like tumbleweed as cold air from the open door comes in. It stinks in here too. Stinks of what I imagine stale mouse droppings would smell like, as well as something burnt.

Once Jay has closed the door behind him and tapped a code into a modern-looking control panel on the wall, he finally turns to both of us. 'This is the Strand entrance to Aldwych tube station, once a part of the Piccadilly line, but essentially defunct since 1994. We commandeered the entire site when it became available and developed it into an expanded base for Vigil London. Above the ticket hall are some of our offices, and below us the complex comprises all the old disused tunnels that once served the tube. With some adaptations.'

Erica and I look around the disgusting space and then back at each other. This really doesn't look like the entrance to a top-secret superhero base. But maybe that's the point.

'This place is known to governments around the world as the Strand, owing to our location,' Jay continues. 'Primary access is through this ticket hall, but there are also access points at Holborn tube station and Temple tube, through the tunnels, should this entrance be compromised.' He turns to Erica alone. 'Don't worry – you'll get a full induction.'

Jay takes out a mobile phone from his jeans pocket and calls someone. The things he says are mostly in code, but I do pick up one phrase: 'She's here too.' I force away the feeling that I should have offered to stay back, because I'm pretty certain that I definitely should be here. I won't let this stupid boy with his stupid coat make me feel uncomfortable. Erica wants me here; therefore I should be here.

'OK, this is where we split up,' Jay says. 'I've had my orders. Louise, we're going to take you upstairs to the office. You can stay there while I take Erica down to the tunnels.'

'She can't come with?' Erica asks.

'She doesn't have the right security clearance. Orders are orders.'

'Don't worry, Lou,' Erica reassures me as I slump and sigh. 'We'll be back really soon, I promise.'

'So what's in the offices upstairs then?' I ask Jay.

'All the most essential parts of the operation: payroll, accounts, HR and general admin.' Despite calling it 'the most essential', he doesn't exactly sound enthused.

'How long will you be downstairs?'

'It's just a quick tour, a meeting or two.' He smiles at Erica, who's avoiding my gaze. 'The preliminary stuff.'

He punches a code into another keypad, by a door that leads off from the ticket hall, then places his thumb to a thumbprint reader. When a light above the reader flicks green, the door creaks open, revealing a narrow staircase. Jay indicates that we're to head upwards, and as we ascend he checks that the door is properly closed behind us. He tells us that the public entrance to the offices is around the back – we're just going this way as it's more convenient right now.

On the first floor, a pristine, middle-aged woman is sitting at a desk. She seems busy typing at her computer, but stops and beams at us as we approach. Behind her glasses her eyes sparkle with excitement, and as we get closer she clacks her artificially elongated fingernails together so that they sound almost mechanical.

'Ladies,' Jay says, 'this is Somnia. Somnia – Erica Elland, and her friend Louise.'

'Erica!' Somnia gushes in a soft voice. 'I am so pleased to finally meet you! I've been keeping track, you know!'

'Thank you! Sonya, was it?'

'No, sweetheart, Somnia. You know, like sleep? Some of us prefer to go by our codenames at work, save what's written on our birth certificates for home. You must understand.'

'Somnia requires absolutely no sleep, and so makes the perfect office administrator. She's like a mum to all of us here,' Jay says. 'Any issues with payroll, or paid leave, or tax issues, just come to her.'

'Oh, hush you! I'm a glorified receptionist and tea maker,' Somnia says, blushing, and then she turns back to Erica. 'But if there is anything I can do for you, sweetness, just let me know. I can make things happen, if you know what I mean!'

'Thank you,' Erica says, obviously charmed.

'And you're Louise Kirby, are you?' Is it my imagination, or do her eyes deaden when she looks at me? Even though I'm standing and she's sitting, it's as if she's looking down her nose at me.

'Don't worry, she's cleared Code Blue. She's to stay up here while we're downstairs,' Jay explains as he hands Somnia the contract. 'We'll be back in a couple of hours. I'm sure there's something Louise can help you with...?'

'Oh, I'll find something!' Somnia trills, but I feel nervous.

As Erica and Jay head back down the stairs I can't help but wonder whether they are relieved to get rid of me. I know Jay would be – he hates the fact that I'm here at all – but there's something in Erica's casual manner that suggests she's now regretting bringing me along.

'So...' Somnia's tone has completely changed, her voice suddenly a lot lower, 'you're the sidekick, huh?' She couldn't sound more disapproving.

'I guess,' I mumble, even though I meant it to come out a lot bolder.

'Well, I suppose it's sweet of you to come here too. Inconvenient, but sweet.' Somnia stands up, and I realise that we're about the same height. She's round like an apple, and wearing clothes that are far too tight for her. Still, there's something in her glare that makes her scarily imposing. 'Now, I don't know what Jay was thinking, bringing you up to me. He knows full well that I can't let you anywhere near the files, no matter what emergency clearance code you've been given. But I suppose we can find you a computer and let you do some homework or something.'

'I didn't bring any homework with me.'

'Of course you didn't.' Somnia looks me up and down, arms crossed over her ample chest. 'Well, perhaps we can show you where the kitchen is. You do know how to make tea and coffee, right?'

I follow her up to the second floor, which is laid out as an open-plan office, shabby and decades old. I wonder whether I have stepped back in time somehow, into a world that's totally colourless and mundane. This is definitely not what I imagined a superhero base to look like. Half the people sitting at the desks look bored, and the other half look like they're nearly asleep.

'Are the people here all right?' I whisper to Somnia.

'This is the accounts department, darling. These people are regulars, just like you. They spend their whole days looking at spreadsheets, assessing targets and working out budgets. You'd look like them too if you were doing the same.'

As we walk through the office nobody even looks up. Somnia takes me to a room at the back, which has a kitchenette on one side and a coffee table and soft seating on the other. There's a small TV fixed to the wall and a water cooler bubbling in the corner; the bubbles sound like mocking laughter.

'I'll leave you here. You can watch the promotional video if you want. Just remember we're busy people in this place. Try not to get in anyone's way.' Without checking if I even want to watch the video, Somnia sets the TV so that it starts playing. Then she turns on her kitten heels and trots back across the office and downstairs to her desk. I sit on one of the couches, uncomfortable and stuffed with stiff industrial foam, and try not to notice the grime in the kitchen.

'We all think our children are special, but what if they were *super*-special?' a happy American voice chirps while the screen flicks through images of smiling children playing. 'So you've just discovered that your son or daughter can do things the other kids can't? Well, don't worry – we at Vigil Corps are here to make things easier. Whether they're super-fast, psychic or able to breathe underwater, the team at Vigil Corps are trained to help, understand and fulfil your child's true potential!' The image flicks to the familiar face of Solar, the leader of the

New York Vigil team, in his trademark gold suit, mask and cape. The close-up manages to keep the logos of his main sponsor just in shot.

'Hi. I'm Solar. I was twelve and living on the streets when I discovered that I could emit full-spectrum light rays from my body. Vigil Corps trained me and taught me to use my talents for good, and if it wasn't for them I'd be off the rails and pursuing a life of crime.' His smile surpasses cheesy. 'By putting your child in the capable hands of the team at Vigil Corps, you can ensure that they get the best start in life and are ready to lead a life of truth, justice and peace.'

'Vigil Corps understands your concerns.' The American lady's voiceover is back, this time over images of smiling superheroes standing on mountain tops, capes billowing behind them. 'We want to assure you that only *we* understand what it's like to be super-special and can provide the best opportunities for your loved one.'

I'm treated to an image of a man in swimming trunks giving the camera a thumbs-up while underwater in some kind of tank – as he turns to the side you can see what I presume are actual fish gills in his neck, allowing him to breathe underwater. Next, a skinny woman in sportswear lifting a car by one of its front wheels while smiling as if she's lifting a feather, and finally an image of a happy scientist shaking hands with Solar, his smile still beaming. It doesn't say why or what for. I know that this video is meant to make me feel content and proud, but there's something about the saccharine sheen, coupled with all the decidedly unsubtle corporate sponsor logos that appear in the background of most of the shots, that just makes me feel uneasy, even a little worried.

Erica must be deep underground within the complex now, mingling with superheroes and getting introduced to all sorts of powerful people. I feel lost in this bland little room with nothing but a half-dead spider plant for company. I'm alone, bored and stuck in this dingy kitchen with a troop of strange adults outside, none of whom look particularly interesting or interested in me. Do they wonder why I'm here? Do Jay and Somnia think I'm sad, following Erica around like a deluded groupie with no life of her own? Without Erica I'm absolutely nothing, and that horrible, plunging feeling that I've been fighting all day finally finds its way up to my throat and lodges there, an undignified lump.

11

'Where were you today?'

Toby is standing outside my house. It's four in the after-noon, I've just got home and there's another hour before my parents will be back from work. I stop a few paces before I reach him, mittened hands stuffed in my pockets, willing my bobble hat to fall over my face. What the hell is he doing here?

'You called in sick to school. But you're blatantly not sick. Where were you?' he asks.

'I was out.'

'Erica wasn't in school today either. Were you with her?'

'What is this? The Spanish Inquisition?'

'No. But you lied. You bunked off. And I even brought you soup.' He holds out a rectangular Tupperware, filled with what looks like a light brown broth. 'Come on, Louise. What's going on? Do your parents know that you skipped school?'

'Leave it, Toby.'

'No.'

He's following me up my driveway as I go to take my house keys out of my bag.

'What the hell are you doing?' I ask as he gets closer to me, so close that I don't know when he's going to stop.

'Are you in trouble? Is Erica?'

'Toby. Leave it now, please.' He steps back, frustrated and obviously wanting to say something else.

'I got your teachers to email your work to you,' he says with a sigh.

'Thanks.'

'I suppose you don't even need the soup.'

If I was Erica I'd invite Toby inside to share the soup with me. We'd sit at my kitchen table, and he'd tell me what I missed in school, and what Mrs Fraser was like at lunchtime without me there. We'd flirt a bit, and maybe he'd ask me out to the cinema again to make up for our aborted attempt last time. But I'm not Erica, and he seems monumentally pissed off at me, and I'm feeling deflated after a spectacularly boring day.

I waited in that office for nearly three hours before Somnia came to give me the message that Erica was still in meetings and I had to keep waiting. I found an ancient stack of magazines in one of the kitchen cupboards, and eventually I was allowed on a computer, but only after a technician had dropped by to make sure that there was no way I could possibly access any important files.

The train home was equally frustrating: Erica couldn't tell me a thing. She wanted to – she was practically bursting with it – but every time I caught her doing that little jump that signalled she was about to explode with gossip, she quickly shut herself up again.

'You should have seen all the stacks of forms that I had to sign,' she explained. 'It's like, proper international government stuff. If I tell anybody anything, I think they can throw me in jail or something.'

'It's all right. I understand,' I said.

'And we did talk about you.'

'What did you say?'

'I can't tell you.'

'Well, then, that's great.'

'Look, the one thing I can tell you is that you have to be careful. I don't think that they're too happy with you being so involved, and of course I told them where to stick it on that front, but – what was the phrase Jay used? Something about an "unknown variable"?'

'You're telling me I have to be careful but you can't tell me why or how or anything else?'

'You know that it's not my choice. I told them that I wanted to tell you everything, that I want you to stay involved.'

'And how did they respond to that?'

'Not too well.'

'Great.'

'They do want me to take my exams though – can you believe it? So even if stuff is going on, it can't happen properly until this coming summer. Until then, we carry on as normal. I mean, I'll be going into town at weekends for training and meetings, so maybe I'll still need help with homework and revision and stuff, but don't you see? Nothing really has to change at all.'

I know Erica thought that she was being generous in what she was telling me, but I was just even more confused and annoyed by it all. There was so much I wanted to ask her, like how they ran their operations, and who made decisions, and how they all kept in touch. Only all the things we'd both been wondering about for the last couple of years.

Now Toby's looking at me, and I know that if I invite him in I'll just be too tempted to tell him everything. So I say, 'No, I don't need the soup,' and turn away.

'Oh. I thought we were good friends, you know? Guess I was wrong.'

He sighs and heads back down my driveway. I feel my heart tug after him. I don't want him to hate me, and I'm sure that I'll figure out some way of making it up between us, but my secrets are pressing too near the surface right now for me to be near anyone, in case they spill out.

'Sorry,' I whisper, but he's too far away to hear.

It's another two weeks before Erica and I discuss anything

Vigil again. Two weeks of pseudo-normality, where we pretend that nothing has happened. We can't talk about it. We see less of each other because there's no reason for her to come over to my house now, and for the first time in a long while I've got only my homework to worry about. I've even got the time to start knitting a new scarf.

I kind of hoped that maybe, when I went back into school and saw Toby again, he would have conveniently forgotten about my truancy. There was a good chance, in my head at least, that we would pretend nothing remotely unusual had happened, and life could continue as normal. No such luck. He's really angry. He's stiff and formal when he's around me now, and I know that what he wants is an apology and an explanation, but I just can't give them. So he remains frosty. Civilised, but definitely frosty.

So at school I'm feeling increasingly lonely because of Toby, and at home too I'm starting to miss Erica.

'Hi, Lou!' She comes up behind me. At first I don't recognise her voice: my brain literally can't compute the idea of Erica being in the library at lunchtime of her own volition.

'Is everything all right?' I ask. I automatically look at her hands, checking for that familiar heat shimmer she gets when she's panicking or stressed.

'Everything's fine!' she chirps, but I don't quite believe her. I sense Toby eyeing us from a couple of stacks away so I walk her over to the reference corner. 'So, I was wondering if you wanted to come to mine after school today.'

'Really?'

'Really. We need a catch-up.'

'Definitely,' I agree.

'Um . . . also, Lou? Why is Toby looking at me like that?'

I turn round and catch him hiding back behind a bookcase, trying to look oblivious. He does a terrible job of it.

'He thinks you're a bad influence on me,' I whisper to her. 'Like you're trying to corrupt me or something.'

'He so blatantly fancies you,' Erica giggles.

'Shhh . . . no, he doesn't. He's just annoyed that I won't tell him why I wasn't in school the other week.'

'And because he fancies you.'

'Shut up,' I hiss.

'Look, I'll wait for you at the gate after school and we'll go over to mine. Mum should be out, so we can chat properly, OK?'

The rest of the day seems to drag on much longer than it should, but then by the time I meet her at the gate Erica isn't so chirpy any more. She's nervous, playing with her fingers as we walk, and doesn't seem to know what she wants to say.

'So, how's your mum?' I dare to ask.

'Oh, you know. Same old.'

'Have you told her anything about you-know-what?'

123

'No. Jeez, can you imagine?'

'But she has to find out about it at some point, right?'

'At some point, yes. But not yet. Right now, all she knows is that I've got a boyfriend who lives in town, and it's not as if she saw much of me before anyway.'

'Is that what Jay is? Your boyfriend?'

'It's complicated.'

Erica shuts up after that and I know better than to press her. Still, I may be totally naive about boys and stuff, but I can't say that Erica seems especially happy. If Jay really was her boyfriend now, however inappropriate that might be, I'd expect her to be much more *Erica-like* about it. Instead, I can't help but think she seems defeated.

'So, there is this one thing I am allowed to talk to you about,' she reveals as we get to her house. 'But I had to absolutely beg to be able to show you, so you can't say a word about it to anyone.' I give her a pointed look, which I hope says *As if you even need to say that*.

The house is all locked up, which I guess means that Liza isn't around, but Erica doesn't say where she is. When we get inside I notice a stockpile of empty wine bottles by the door.

'That's for recycling,' Erica mumbles.

It smells different in here too. There's a mustiness that I never noticed before, like how a coat smells if it's been hanging up in a closet for too long and hasn't had any air. Peeking through to the kitchen, I can see a mountain of washing-up and a couple of baskets overflowing with dirty clothes next to the washing machine. The bin needs taking out, but instead of dealing with it, it looks like the rubbish is just being piled on a nearby countertop.

'Erica?' I start, but then I let the question trail off because I don't know what to say.

We head up to her room, where she proceeds to quickly close her curtains before reaching over to her iPod speakers and setting the volume of her music insanely high.

'What are you doing?' I ask over the top of some vintage Britney Spears (Erica has a severe weakness for Millennial pop).

'Just taking some precautions,' she shouts back. 'Jay's taught me a lot about personal security. I have to be careful now.'

She pulls out a box from down the side of her desk, in a place that's partially hidden by stacks of fashion and celebrity magazines. It's a large, flat box, and Erica handles it like it contains something immensely precious. We both sit on her bed, the box between us, and the Britney song is now playing so loud that the lyrics are distorted into angry, auto-tuned mewls. Erica stares at me and takes a deep breath before finally opening the lid.

Inside is a suit. A supersuit. Her costume. Erica unfolds it and holds it up against her so that I can see the shape. It's black, and obviously tight, in fact it looks strikingly similar to the suit that I made, except this one is made of expensive materials and has fancy stitching. It looks so professional and real. I feel that my costume was just a toddler's doodle compared to this, a proper work of art. I wish I could make something like this. I wish I *had* made it.

Erica grabs a notepad and starts scrawling down a message in front of me: It's a prototype. Isn't it cooooool?!?!?!?!?!

Once I've read it, Erica tears off the paper and scrunches it up, before allowing a ball of fire in her hands to consume the note and make it disappear like the final wisp of a paper ghost. Then she signals she's going to show me something more. Rubbing her thumb and forefingers together to kindle a gentle flame, she places her hand down onto the torso of the suit. I can see that her hand is burning hot, it's actually glowing red, but when she takes it away the material of the suit is utterly unscathed. Erica gestures for me to touch the part of the suit she just attempted to fry, and I reach down warily and let my fingertips touch it before pulling my hand away, expecting a burn. But there is none. I try again, this time allowing my whole palm to rest on the patch of material that should be scorched or molten. But it's cool. It's completely cool.

Erica writes another note: This is astronaut material. It's practically indestructible!!!!

Once again she quickly tears up the note and lets it burn to ashes.

'We can't talk about this, ever. OK?' Erica shouts at me. I make the international sign-language gesture for *My lips are sealed*. She continues: 'Because actually, even though I know that I'm allowed to tell you about this, I might not necessarily have been given authorisation to *show* you.'

I grab the notepad, prepared to demonstrate exactly how much I understand how sensitive this all is, and write down: *It looks amazing!!!! And I can already imagine it covered in sponsor logos, just like a real Vigil uniform!!!!!!*

Erica writes back to me: *Wouldn't it be nice if the suit wasn't going to be covered in logo patches? If it was just me? And that stood for enough?*

Me: *That's not how it works.*

Erica sighs and lets her hand trail over the futuristic black fabric, caressing it like a beloved pet. Her other hand clasps the piece of paper we were just writing on, and it vaporises completely within her hot fist. We sit closer together on the bed, so that even though the music is still loud we can just about hear each other when we talk.

'Will you get in trouble for showing it to me?' I ask. I figure if I'm not being too specific, talking instead of note-writing will be all right.

'Not if they don't find out. Jay says I have to learn to cut my ties with the past and look to the future. He thinks it's all waiting for me, if I can just let go. Except, I just felt, after everything we've been through, I couldn't not show you. You know?'

'Do you do everything Jay says?'

'He's what they call my "handler". Everything has to go through him first. He's my first call. It sucks that he's not in school any more, but he says that he has other work to do, so I get it. We talk nearly every night though. He's really sweet.'

'What do you talk about?' I try to make it sound casual, and hope that her Jay obsession will hide the fact that I'm totally prying and suspicious.

'He has these big ideas. About life, the universe, but mostly about the Vigils. He was so impressed when I told him that my favourite is the Amazing Clara, because he said that most girls nowadays wouldn't get what she was about. We talk about this –' she gestures to the suit between us – 'and how it would be so great if there was no such thing as sponsors. Being a Vigil now is so much about the money – but back then, when the Amazing Clara was saving the world, it was all about selflessness and justice. He calls them the "golden days". Says that he'd love to bring them back, and how, you know, when I get old enough to join the team properly, that I could do a lot of good for the world.'

'He has a lot of faith in you.'

'Really he's just amazing. And, I know I can tell you this

and you won't laugh or anything, but I think he's just waiting for me to get older, and complete my training, and then we can be together. He's putting no pressure on me. He knows how important joining the Vigils is. Look, I'll show you something else...'

Erica leaves my side, eyes ablaze with mischief, and goes back over to her desk. She puts the costume away, then reaches into the back of a drawer and pulls out a scrap of paper. Then she comes back to the bed.

'I have to be really careful not to burn it or anything,' she admits, handing the scrap to me.

It's a portrait of Erica, absolutely perfect, right down to the way her hair falls on one side. It looks like it's been done with the finest of ink pens.

'Jay's really good at the whole photocopying thing,' she says. 'But this is where his superpower gets really special. All he did was look at me, and then put his hand down on the paper, and suddenly this picture was there. It was like he saw me, *really* saw me.'

'Wow,' I mouth.

'It's the most romantic thing anyone has ever done for me.'

I admit that I'm impressed, even though the whole thing makes me feel a little icky, and then offer to put the portrait back away for her. Erica reaches over to her sound system and turns the music down. I guess that means the superhero chat is over. On her desk is a recent English essay. We're in different classes for English but I had the same assignment last week.

'You got a D on this? But we read the book together. I thought you liked it.' I'm a little perplexed at the result – she should have done a lot better.

'Whatever.' Erica doesn't seem interested.

'But you definitely could have got a B, maybe even an A. What happened? Why didn't you ask me for help?'

'Lou, I'm going to be a Vigil. Who cares about animal imagery in the characterisation of Lennie in *Of Mice and Men*?'

'Didn't they say they wanted you to get your grades too?'

'Jay told me that they say that to all the new recruits. It's just in case you don't end up being strong enough for the A team and have to end up doing a desk job or research work or something. But that's not going to happen with me. He says I'm a shoo-in for the A team, so I figured, what's the point of bothering with the exams?'

'You need at least a C in English . . .' I start, thinking about the requirements for the sixth form at our school.

'Well, if you're going to be a regular person, yes. But I'm not a regular person. I'm going to be a Vigil. Trust me, Lou, everything is going to be fine.'

I wish I could trust her. I really do. But as I walk home after sunset through the dark streets, I feel nervous. I want to walk right up to Jay and ask him what the hell he thinks he's doing. I know that grades might not be everything to Erica but he can't make her blow her exams off. What happens if she gets injured one day and needs something to fall back on? I wonder if maybe I'm just feeling funny about all of this because I'm not involved. Suddenly Erica has yet another secret life, one that I'm not a part of this time, and as much as I'm trying to be happy for her, it's just not happening.

12

How long has it been since we were both at the tunnel together, just the two of us? A month? Miraculously the stub of Jay's cigarette is still there, just inside the tunnel entrance, protected from the weather by the brickwork. I know it's just one stub, but I feel as if this place has been polluted. If I had a dustpan and brush handy, I'd be all over it. We're here in the daytime for a change. A rare Sunday off for Erica means she wants me to traipse along after her and witness all the new tricks she's learned. So here I am, a miserable lackey, carrying her stuff and thinking about all the other things that I could be getting on with, while Erica does her Excited-Child thing.

I'm getting horribly used to this. And I know I was never all that enthusiastic about our little tunnel adventures to begin with, especially after dark, but at least I was still a part of things. Erica needed me, whether to give her encouragement, to praise her, or to help her keep her feet – metaphorically – on the ground. But now? She just wants to show off. It doesn't matter what I think or say, she's craving an audience. I'm second-rate compared to her new friends, someone she feels that she needs to clock in time with to stave off the guilt. Well, I think she should feel guilty. It may not be entirely her fault, but still, I feel it.

'You know they've got me training properly now, like running and everything,' she starts. 'And I'm doing weights to make me stronger because everybody tells me that's a big weakness of mine. Some flyers have super-strength too, like Quantum, but I'm seriously lacking in that area. But then again, Quantum hasn't got fire power. In fact, he's not got anything apart from the flying and the strength, so really I don't know what his big deal is.'

'He's the leader of the London team?' I offer.

'But you know, he's really not all that...I mean, obviously he's Quantum, and he's amazing, but Deep Blue? He's the one with the brains.'

'So have you met everyone, then?'

'Of course I have, silly!' I hate the way she says this, as if it's obvious, but it's not as if she's ever talked about it before. 'I mean, they're always out and about at the weekends, and I'm not, like, officially on the team yet, but I've met pretty much everyone now and they're all super-nice.'

'Are you even allowed to be talking about this with me?'

'Don't worry, the guys have swept this whole area for bugs and stuff. We're totally safe here.'

Who are these 'guys' she's talking about? And why does she just assume that I'd understand exactly what she means? I think about the fact that other people, people that I don't know, must have been here if the tunnel has indeed been *swept*. This place, once our own personal secret hideout, doesn't feel very secret any more.

'So can I show you something?' Erica asks.

'Sure...'

'It's something that I'm practising, but haven't really got down yet. So you'll have to stand back quite a bit.'

'Is it dangerous?'

'Possibly. Probably not... but possibly. It's something I've been thinking about ever since that day at the cinema, and I've been talking to Jay about it but he says I should keep it quiet from the rest of the Vigil guys until I know exactly what I can do, you know? So can I try it in front of you?'

'Of course. But what is it?'

'I'll show you, but come and stand behind me first.'

I get up off the bench and move behind her, while Erica lines herself up in front of a small branch she retrieved from the very top of a tree a bit earlier. Why she couldn't grab a branch nearer the ground, I don't know.

'Is this like the heat-wave thing?' I ask.

'Shh...just watch!'

It starts out like the heat wave, except that the branch is decidedly not on fire to begin with. I can't feel anything

134

from where I'm standing but I can see the air dancing with pulsing heat, shimmering as Erica holds her palm out towards the branch. Her posture tenses as she focuses the heat, and then suddenly the branch bursts into flame. She wasn't even touching it. She doesn't stop. Now it's like the heat wave. The branch is alight and Erica keeps the pulses going so that the flame flares quickly upwards, angry and bright. I have to take a few steps back. The flames are so dazzlingly hot it prickles my skin and forces me to screw up my eyes. At one point I wonder how far this could go – could the branch actually explode from all the energy? Is that what Erica can do now, explode things from a distance? But the flames die back down as the branch completely incinerates to nothing but black ash.

'Wow . . . spontaneous combustion,' I mutter. I'm a little scared. This is a level of power I hadn't even considered Erica capable of before.

'I know, right?' Erica turns back to me, a little out of breath from the exertion but looking incredibly pleased with herself. 'Jay calls me his little bombshell. Get it? *Bomb*shell?'

'You can really set fire to things from a distance.' I say it in disbelief.

'Apparently so! But you know, a puny branch is one thing, I still have no idea how big I can take this!'

She goes out from the tunnel and into the field, so I follow, keeping an eye out for anyone who could be watching in the bright afternoon daylight. She comes to stand in front of a tree, an old oak that, because of its size and because its roots run deep and wide, is alone in the field. It sits apart, like a monument, and I guess that it's been here long before the area was swallowed up by suburbia and its parkland.

'What are you doing?' I ask as I stand behind Erica, who is now holding both her arms out towards the tree. The grass under our feet crunches with dead leaves.

'Was just thinking about how big I could go, and I was wondering...' She trails off.

'Erica? What were you wondering?' My eyes dart from her, to her outstretched hands, to the tree before us. 'Erica!'

I can see the air dancing from the heat she's projecting, and I wonder if this is a joke, if she's just trying to see how far she can go before somebody stops her. Except that she's not listening. She's aiming her powers at this magnificent oak, and I can't just stand here and let her destroy it in the same way that she incinerated that branch.

'Shhh,' Erica mumbles. 'I just want to see...'

I can't let her do this. Apart from the environmental concern, if she sets the tree on fire she'll be alerting people for miles around to our presence here. A great hulk of flaming oak does not go unnoticed. And then what? What if the fire spreads and she can't contain it? Sure, she

can grow flames and manipulate spontaneous combustion, but what happens when the flames get too much?
How does she stop them?

'Erica!' I stand in front of her.

The force of the heat is like a hundred hairdryers
blowing right in my face. It's a jet stream of energy,
pouring off her and onto me in stomach-churning waves.
It takes my breath away and dries my throat. Fortunately
she manages to put her hands down before any real
damage is done, but I'm sweating and struggling to regain
my breath once the November chill finds me again.

'What do you think you're doing?' she demands, as if it
was me who was doing something crazy.

'Stopping you from instigating an ecological disaster!' I
reply, wiping the sweat from my face.

'Oh, come on, I was never going to go through with it!'
She turns and stomps back into the tunnel. I follow close
behind.

I cross my arms and ponder what just happened. I was
terrified. What she did was dangerous and destructive,
and there was something in her eyes, a drunk giddiness,
that made my heart pang with terror. It was like Excited-
Child Mode on turbo-charge. And now, even as she paces
in the tunnel, I can tell she's enjoying all of this a little too
much. Despite my interference, she's still woozy on her
little power trip and bubbling with excess energy. She
needs someone to remind her to use this power for good,

and not to let it get out of hand or to go to her head, but I don't know how to say any of this without making her angry. We're not talking like that any more. I'm not Erica's *handler*.

'Jay says that if I work really hard, maybe I'll be more powerful than Quantum one day.' She's talking as if what just happened was nothing. 'He reckons that I could end up being the first female leader of the London team. Isn't that amazing? I just can't believe this stuff is within my grasp, you know? Can you imagine, me – a Vigil leader?'

'You're still young...' I start to say. I want to add *and inexperienced, and may not even pass some of your GCSEs? Oh, and by the way, YOU JUST NEARLY BLEW UP A WHOLE TREE FOR NO REASON.* But I stop myself, wary that I might set Erica off.

I miss what it used to be like between us, so much. How did I become scared of her?

There was this one time last year when Erica was desperate to get out of a history test, because despite my efforts to help her with the revision, she just couldn't get her head around it.

'What's the point of powers if I can't ever use them to get out of trouble?' she asked me, after which I did my usual job of telling her that it wasn't an important test anyway and she should just muddle through it.

Maybe I should have realised that her desire to push the limits and see what she could do was far more overwhelming than simply admitting defeat in history. Once she's determined to do something, she has to go through with it.

There were these ramshackle prefab huts just on the edge of the school field that had been set up as temporary classrooms decades ago and never taken down. They weren't used for teaching any more, but some after-school clubs were held in them. They had the old-fashioned type of sprinklers set into the ceiling and were rarely patrolled by the prefects or teachers.

So of course Erica had decided that this was the perfect place to make mischief. On the day of the test she went into one of the prefabs just before the end of break and let a hand burn, then flew up to the ceiling and activated the sprinklers. This automatically set off the fire alarm. If she just hit any old fire alarm randomly, someone would soon figure out that everything was fine and life would go on as normal. But what she needed was a big-ass diversion that would put the history test off for a few days and allow her more time to cram. By setting off the sprinklers, she figured that the school would be evacuated and most of the next lesson would certainly be disrupted.

The first I knew about all of this was when I received a text on my phone moments after the alarm started wailing. I was in the library during break – of course I was – and it didn't take me long to put two and two together to get the result: Erica-trouble.

I'm stuck in the outbuilding classroom! COME AND HELP ME!!!!

Those of us in the library shuffled out to the corridor, which was a thronging mass of kids making their way out to the field and the fire assembly point. I quickly veered away towards the outbuildings. For once I was thrilled I was short – nobody noticed me to tell me that I was heading the wrong way. I briefly wondered whether I did have a superpower after all: Super-Stealth Wallflower Mode.

When I finally found her, I had to stop and laugh. Because it was hilarious. Erica, being Erica, hadn't actually planned out her sprinkler stunt too well. For some reason she had committed her prank at the very back of the classroom, meaning that as soon as the water started falling, she was stuck in her position up in the corner next to the ceiling. If she had tried to get out by herself, she would have been totally soaked through, and immediately rumbled.

'Don't just stand there!' she yelled at me, but I was enjoying it all far too much.

Finally, after letting her stew for a suitable amount of time, I took off my blazer, pulled my trusty umbrella out of my bag and opened it over my head before venturing into the classroom. I knew that we didn't have a lot of time before a teacher came to inspect. Once I was close enough, Erica shimmied herself down and under the umbrella with me, and we legged it back outdoors with barely a drop of water hitting either of us.

Sure, we were told off for being a little late to line up on the field for the register, but nothing could beat my sense of satisfaction. Saving Erica had been amazing, and to top it all off, she had got her timetable wrong; history wasn't straight after break, but the lesson before lunch. So the test went ahead as scheduled and Erica flunked spectacularly. It was just brilliant.

'You remember that time with the sprinklers?' I ask Erica as we're walking back through the field.

'How could I forget? You totally saved me that day,' she replies.

I need her to remember this, right now, as our friendship slips away. *I* saved *her.*

'Why did you bring that up?' she asks me, clearly perplexed by my train of thought.

'No reason.'

'Oh, that reminds me,' she says, stopping in her tracks. 'There was something else I wanted to tell you.'

I stop too and stuff my hands in my duffel-coat pockets. I wonder if she's going to apologise for nearly frying me. I wonder if that's even occurred to her.

'So, some people were talking about my name. You know, the whole Flamegirl thing. And it was suggested that maybe it wasn't the greatest codename.'

'What people?'

'Oh, there are like all these people that I meet – branding people, merchandising people, stylists and promoters and all sorts. You wouldn't believe how many people are involved in the whole Vigil thing. Anyway, the Flamegirl name was brought up in a meeting and everybody kind of felt the same as you. That it wasn't really good enough, and they wanted something more original, with more impact.'

'Well, I could have told you that. In fact, I think I *did* tell you that.'

'So, some names were getting thrown around but I didn't like any of them, and then I kinda suggested your idea: Vega. And everybody loved it. So I wanted to tell you before you saw it anywhere, when I get launched, that I'll probably be called Vega now. That's cool, isn't it? I mean, it was your idea originally, so that's really cool, right?'

'But you hated it when I suggested it.'

'Yes, but the branding and merchandising people like it. And Jay really likes it.'

'So you listened to them but not me?'

'Oh, please, don't get all pissy with me about this. It is your idea after all. We're going with your idea! You should be happy about it!'

Erica starts to walk again but I'm too stunned to even move. I can't even explain this bubble of anger that's sitting in me. It's like I don't even know Erica any more. Who is she? If Jay told her to throw herself off a cliff, would she do it? OK, bad example, she can fly – but still. Why is his opinion so much more important than mine? I've been there since the beginning, and what am I getting for it?

This isn't how I thought it was going to go. This isn't what I thought any of this was going to be like.

'Oh, come on, Lou,' Erica says. 'Why are you making such a big deal about this? This is amazing. You should be happy for me.'

'Do I even get credit?' I ask.

'What do you mean?'

'For the costume design, and the name, and whatever else. Do *they* know that it was all me? Do I ever get any credit?'

'You know it doesn't work like that. And besides, I never thought you were the "needing credit" sort.'

'I'm not. It's not about that. It's just…' I try to think of anything I can say that won't result in her getting angry (and potentially literally exploding right here in the park) but can't come up with a thing. I realise the only way to deal with this is to back down, and nurture the hope that somehow everything will work out fine eventually and that I'll start to feel happy again.

'Nothing,' I say finally. 'It's nothing. I am happy. I always thought that Vega was the perfect name and that you'd come around.'

13

I once heard that déjà vu is when the memory cells of your brain cross over each other accidentally, so that something feels familiar even though it's completely brand new. You might get it in a bakery because your brain already has bread-smell memories and can't work out if those memories are new or old. Or an ocean view might remind you of something, and then your brain crosses wires and you think that you must have been right there before. I can understand how it might happen, and how you can convince yourself that you're experiencing the exact same moment for the second time.

Except that I *have* been here before. It's dark and raining outside, and I'm stuck on a maths problem that I just can't get my head around. Suddenly Erica arrives in my room, slamming the door behind her before stopping still, panting and sizzling and looking like she wants to cry and scream at the same time.

'What is it?' I'm on high alert, noticing the warm glow around her fingertips, as soft and fragile as a dying candle flame.

'I can't believe she...Oh my God, my mum! You wouldn't believe...!' Erica holds her hands out, aware that if she presses them behind her she'll likely set fire to my dressing gown hanging on the back of the door.

'OK...OK...slow down. Need me to run you a bath?'

'I'm furious, I'm not a baby!' Erica's tone is unexpectedly sharp, which unnerves me – when we were last here, the ice-cold bath was the best idea I had.

'Erica, I'm only trying to help. And you're on fire, in my room. Can we just calm down for a minute before you burn down my house?' She watches me, jaw tensed and eyes focused, and for the briefest of moments I'm scared of her. 'I'm going downstairs to get you a drink, OK? And then we'll talk.'

When I get back to my room with a large glass of ice from the freezer, Erica is perched on my bed, arms wrapped around her knees. I try to work out if she's crying, because I can't quite see her face, but as I edge nearer I decide that her face is screwed up with rage more than anything else. I don't remember the last time she was this angry. Sure, she can be moody, but this is something else. I reach over to hand her the glass, and she takes it, chucking back the ice chips into her mouth. The ice left in the glass melts in the heat of her grasp.

'So what's going on?' I ask, the déjà vu attacking me again as I settle into my desk chair.

'Mum and I had another fight,' Erica admits. 'I tried to tell her . . . not the whole thing . . . but she was asking about Jay and where I go on the weekends, and I was like, finally! After years of wanting to talk to her, *finally* she's interested in what I'm doing, and I can't tell her a thing! She was yelling at me, and it was ridiculous, and I tried to tell her that Jay was one of the good guys but she just didn't believe me. She thinks I'm going to get pregnant and turn out just like her, so when I told her that Jay's not like that, that he's helping me, she went ballistic. Said I was a fool for trusting someone I've only just met, and that Jay's only after one thing.'

'I'm so sorry,' I say after a pause.

'And I thought, God forbid, if I actually have to tell her what's going on, she's not going to take it. She's not going to believe me, even if I wave my stupid hands right in front of her, because she's so off her face most of the time that she'd just think she was hallucinating or something.'

I want to say something. I want to apologise again, or say something about the wine bottles I saw at her place, or that time when I saw her mum drinking wine from a mug, but the words leave me. This is the one thing that Erica's never talked to me about before. I would never have pried, and she would never have admitted to it.

'She's a monster, you know.' Erica sighs. 'She's always drunk, and has always liked getting drunk, but before she only did it when she was celebrating. Or if she was really

146

sad and wanted to forget. Now it's all the time. And she doesn't think I notice it, but I do. I've watched it for months. And I'm sick of it. My life is finally becoming something. I'm finally getting to do exactly what I've always wanted, and she's ruining it for me.'

I wait for a break so that I can offer more ice, because it's the only thing I can think of to do or say, but the breaks don't come. I can tell that she's working hard at keeping herself controlled, if only for my sake, but maybe we should be heading for the tunnel right now, so she can just let it all go.

'I just can't believe the things she was saying about Jay, and she hasn't even met him! Saying that I shouldn't be thinking about boys right now because of my exams, and if I absolutely had to think about boys then I should at least be thinking about boys my own age. Jay is only a few years older than us! Hardly anything, really! And screw exams! I don't need them. I'll never need them, and I don't know why the Vigils won't just let me move to London and be a part of the team now, because Jay says I'm ready for it. Exams will just hold me back!'

I don't think I'm hiding the doubt from my face very well, because suddenly Erica stares right at me and says, 'What?'

'Nothing,' I reply.

'No. I can tell that you want to say something. What is it? Just get it out.'

'You're scary like this, Erica,' I mumble.

'For goodness sake, Louise. If I can't talk to you about all this, then who *can* I talk to? Whatever you want to say to me, just say it.'

I think about lying. I think about saying whatever I can to make her calm down. I could tell her how wonderful she is, and how she just has to be patient, and that maybe my mum will allow her to move in with us for the time being, but it's just not right. I don't want to lie to Erica to make her happy. That's not why I'm her friend. She might hate me right now for saying it, but in the long run she'll appreciate that I always told her the truth. Won't she?

'What is it?' Erica insists.

'I'm just not sure about Jay. There's something about him, and the things he says to you, that just doesn't feel right.' It feels like such a relief to say the words out loud to her, but it's quickly squashed by the look on her face.

'You are joking me,' she says.

'I know it's not what you want to hear but I'm just not sure about him.'

'We're really going down this road, after everything I just told you about my mum?'

'I'm not saying that your mum is right, and by the sounds of it I get that you've been having a horrible time with her, but if you're really asking me what I think about everything, well . . . I think that Jay's not right.'

I look down at my rug while Erica glares at me. Her being angry with me is the last thing I want, but right now the truth seems so much more important, especially as I've spent most of my spare time over the last couple of weeks thinking and stressing about this very issue. No matter how hard she makes it for me, I know that this might be my very last chance to tell Erica what I really think before I lose her.

'You've barely spent any time with him!'

'He hates me.'

'And you think it's all right to just hate him back?'

'No, it's not just that. It's the things he says to you, and how you've changed. It's like you're becoming a whole new person, with this costume and the secret meetings at weekends. I've hardly seen you since we went down to London. And when I do see you, you scare me. I'm not sure that I like what you're becoming.'

'You were round at mine last week! I showed you the costume! Do you know how hard it was for me to get that out for you? How much effort I had to make just to try and keep you involved? And what about the park last weekend? You're just throwing it right back at me, trying to make me feel guilty for following my dream!'

'I'm sorry, I just . . . This is just how I feel, OK?'

She's standing up now, pacing around in what little space there is between my bed and my window. I keep myself as small and tucked in as possible on my chair, scared that she might pounce out at me on a whim with her angry burning hands. They're not ablaze now, but I can tell that they want to be, that she's using every tiny bit of her strength to hold herself back.

'I knew it,' she mutters, stopping and staring blankly out of my window.

'Knew what?'

'You're jealous. This is what it's all been about since the beginning. You're jealous of me.'

'What? No!'

'You might not have been at first, but now . . . now that the Vigils are taking me in, you're scared of being left behind. What – you think that Jay is taking me away from you? Can't deal with the fact that I have new, better friends now?'

'Erica, you're my best friend.'

'You *were* my best friend.' Her words stun me. 'You were the one person I trusted above everyone. I wouldn't even be where I am without you. But now what? Can't handle the fact that I'm leaving you behind?'

I'm starting to feel angry now too. I shouldn't be acting the meek and modest little girl in her chair, all wrapped up and small. This is *my* room, and she's my friend that I'm trying to protect. I shouldn't have to just sit here and listen to her say horrible things to me while I do nothing to protect myself. If Erica wants a full-blown blazing row, then it looks like I'm going to be giving it to her.

'Fine,' I start, noticing that my breathing feels tight and heavy, that my voice sounds cracked and bruised. 'You know what? If we're going there, then yes, I'll tell you the truth. I don't know who you are any more. The Erica I used to know wouldn't accuse me of the things you've just said. She'd know without me even having to say it that I loved her and wanted the best for her. I still do. We both know that Jay hates me, so let's think about what he might be saying to you, to turn you against me. Can you just think about that for even a moment?'

'Jay is a Vigil. He's one of them. He's one of the good guys,' Erica replies, and for the first time, I get her logic. How could one of the Vigils be wrong?

'Well, he's never seemed like a particularly good guy to me. I don't trust him. All right?' I realise that I'm not going to win this. That even though Jay is miles away wherever he lives, somehow he's got Erica completely on his side.

'You're wrong, Louise. You don't even realise how wrong you are. My whole life is opening up in front of me, and you're trying to destroy it. Just like my mum. I always thought I had you, Louise. I might never have had her, but I always thought I had *you*.' She moves to open my window.

'Where are you going?'

'I'm getting out of here before I burn your whole bloody house down. Isn't that what you want?'

'We can talk more . . .'

'I've got nothing more to say to you. I'm going.'

'But you have to go back out the front door, otherwise my mum might wonder how—'

'Like I care about that any more. You think I have time any more to wonder whether your mum notices how I come and go?'

I want to remind her how kind my mum has always been, how she's always welcomed Erica without question. That if she leaves from my window, it will open up questions and lead to lies. Weirdly, in my head, this simple act seems just as horrifying and tragic as any words she could possibly say.

After she's gone, I'm sitting on my bed in the very same spot where she was just minutes ago, and it still feels warm. I haven't got the head for my maths homework now. Maybe I should be crying but I'm too stunned. Each gust of wind that rattles my window pane makes me look up, hoping that Erica has come back to apologise. But the rain pounds on outside and I feel lost and empty.

It's as I'm getting ready for bed that I notice the parcel on my bedside table. Mum must have left it there for me. I can guess what it is. Maybe I should just throw it straight in the bin now and avoid the feelings. Or maybe I should scratch out my address on the front and forward it straight to Erica, so that she can incinerate it. If I was brave I might ask her for the money to cover what I've already laid out for it, but we've never been that pernickety about money before. We always shared costs equally because we shared the experience equally. But now here it is, a reminder of what I don't have any more. It's the Halloween costume I ordered from America, all ready to be turned into Erica's new superhero costume.

14

Nobody has seen Erica for a week. Not since our blow-out. She's not been in school. I don't know what to say about that. Some of her friends have come up to me in break and at lunchtime to ask if I've spoken to her, and I play it as though I'm clueless. Of course I'm thinking that she must be in London, playing with Jay and her new Vigil buddies, but I can't tell anybody that. All I can do is shrug my shoulders apologetically and go back to whatever it is I'm doing.

Until Friday, when I get called out of my English lesson.

'Note for Louise Kirby to see Mr Stanley,' says the Year Seven kid, a shrunken shrimp within her oversized school blazer. The teacher dismisses me amid a hushed wave of 'umms' and 'oohs', as if I'm in trouble.

As I follow the tiny Year Seven, so proud of her incredibly important job, I consider making a run for it. I know what this is about. But what am I meant to say?

Yeah, sorry Mr Deputy Head, but Erica has abandoned all hopes of a decent education by running away to join a troupe of superheroes. Like that's going to go down well. I figure that I'll just have to play coy like I've been doing with everyone else, and hope that my poker face is good enough to hold up against the scrutiny of an authority figure.

What I'm not expecting when I finally get into the deputy head's office, is for Liza to be there. Mr Stanley is there too, sitting behind his desk with his head poised thoughtfully on a tense fist, but I barely notice him. It's Liza who captures my attention, with her gaunt frame and pale face, made somehow paler by her blonde hair, which is scraped back and forced into an untidy bun. She's wearing a tracksuit that might once have been white but is now grey, and the half-fastened zip directs my eye to her collarbone, which protrudes painfully. Liza has always been thin, but right now she looks as scrawny as a baby deer, so different from her athletic daughter.

'Come and sit down, Louise, and don't be nervous,' Mr Stanley directs, and I do as I'm told. No chance of running away now.

'You're good friends with Erica Elland, am I right?' Mr Stanley asks, and I nod in reply, too scared to say anything in case I somehow incriminate myself. 'We were just wondering if you've seen Erica at all this week, or even spoken to her. She's not been in school since Monday. Have you heard from her?'

'She's not spoken to me,' I reply, mouth dry.

'Would you have any idea where she might be?' While Mr Stanley talks, Liza's eyes are wide and searching.

'No. We had a fight last week. I've not heard from her since.'

Mr Stanley sits back in his big desk chair and ponders this revelation. 'What did you fight about?' he asks, his tone soft, like he's trying to coax something out of me.

'Oh, you know, boys.' I shrug.

'It was after she fought with me, wasn't it?' Liza sighs. 'I knew it. I drove her away. And now she's gone.'

'You haven't heard from her?' I ask. Although I expected her to give me the silent treatment, I hardly considered that Erica would stay away from her mum too. However much they fought, Erica would never just leave.

'We've called the police. Reported her missing,' Liza mumbles from dry lips.

'The police?' I echo.

'They'll want to talk to you, but they're checking in with her father first.'

Mr Stanley fiddles with a pen on his desk, clicking it as though somehow that might diffuse the tension. I wonder whether the police are able to do anything. Would they interfere with Vigil business? Would they be allowed to tell Liza and Mr Stanley what's going on if the Vigils did talk to them?

'I think she's with her father. She must have gone to him.' Liza turns to Mr Stanley. 'We've been fighting. More so than usual. It's never been easy, but you must under-stand – teenage girls, right? Anyway, she used to talk a lot about going to stay with her dad, but I never thought that she'd just up and leave. She drives me mad, but all I ever want is the best for her. Why doesn't she see that?'

If Erica was here, she'd argue back that her mum has no idea what's best for her. It plays out in my head as if she really was here, but I stay quiet, for if ever there was a time for shutting up, this is it. I'm relieved that they think that Erica is with her father, but once the police realise that's not the case, what then? Maybe I should find a way to get through to her, just to let her know that people are worrying and that she has to cover herself. Then hopefully this whole thing will blow over and be forgotten by next week.

'There's been this new boyfriend too. Do you know anything about that?' Liza asks me.

'Not really...' I lie. I hate lying.

'I told her that she shouldn't be getting involved with boys. Not at her age. Not when so much schoolwork needs doing, and not when she has so much potential. She can't go around making the same mistakes I did. I won't have it. And he's older too – did you know that, Mr Stanley?'

'Yes, well, about this boy—' Mr Stanley starts.

'He goes here,' I interrupt. 'His name is Jay...' It's only then that I realise I have no idea what his last name is.

'Except that he doesn't,' Mr Stanley takes over. 'He enrolled in our sixth form at the beginning of term, but then took himself off-register a few weeks ago. Do you know anything about that?'

'No...'

'You think this Jay person has something to do with Erica going away?' Liza asks Mr Stanley.

He turns to me, as if I might have the answers.

'I didn't like him...' I say carefully. 'We fought about that too.'

'Is there any chance that Erica might be with him right now, and not at her dad's?' Mr Stanley asks.

'I really couldn't say. I don't know.' I will the conversation to end, because I know that if I start talking about Jay and who he really is, everything else will start to unravel too. Is there any way I can tell them that I'm sure Erica is all right without giving away any specific details?

'Louise, if there is anything that you can tell us at this point, then it would be incredibly helpful. We're all concerned about Erica's wellbeing, so if you're protecting her –' Mr Stanley uses his hands a lot as he talks – 'now is the time to come forward and tell us what you know.'

'I don't know anything,' I insist. 'We had an argument, and I haven't heard from her since.'

Except now, instead of thinking she's run away to the Vigils out of spite, I'm wondering if something more sinister is happening. No matter how I look at this whole situation,

I just can't believe Erica would choose to totally disappear. Because didn't the Vigils want her to stay in school? Wouldn't they just escort her back to her mum's house if she turned up on their doorstep looking for sanctuary? I'd at least expect them to get in touch, or to figure out some way of letting Liza know that everything is fine. Leaving me in the lurch, fair enough – it's not as if they've ever reached out an olive branch to me – but to make Liza so scared; that doesn't make any sense. And now there's the police to deal with. Lying to the deputy head is one thing, but lying to the law? I don't think I could ever handle that. I'm growing increasingly cold as I think about what might be going on, and whether Erica really is safe right now.

'OK, thanks for your help, Louise,' Mr Stanley says. 'The police will be in touch shortly. If you hear anything from Erica, please come and let us know.'

I'm dismissed, and I feel rotten.

I dig my phone out of my pocket and call Erica. As the phone rings, and rings, I steal away into the nearby girls' toilets so that nobody can see or hear me. I even do that thing I've only ever seen on cop shows and in films, checking under the door of each cubicle to see if anyone is hiding. I'm definitely alone.

'Come on, Erica . . . pick up the phone . . .' I mutter.

I send her a quick message when I realise that nobody is picking up: *Where are you??? Are you OK?????*

I try ringing once more, telling myself that I'll leave a

voicemail for her. She might still hate me, but she'd hate me more if I just let her mum and the school declare her a Missing Person without telling her about it.

The line picks up but I don't hear Erica on the other end.

'Hello? Erica? Are you there?' Nobody says anything. I take the phone away from my ear so that I can see if the line is still connected. It is. 'Erica? Erica, can you hear me? Where are you?'

'You really need to stop interfering with situations that just don't involve you.' I recognise Jay's voice.

'Where's Erica?' I demand.

'This is none of your business any more.'

'What's going on, Jay? Please, just tell me what's going on.'

'Relax. Erica's with me. There's no need to worry.'

'Then let me speak to her.'

'I'm afraid she's busy right now. But I can take a message?'

I can feel him sneering down the line, and I rub at the back of my neck to try to stop the slimy feeling creeping over me.

'Erica's been declared missing. She needs to come home, or at least let somebody know that she's all right. Please let me speak to her.'

'I told you. Erica's busy. And she doesn't want to speak to you right now.'

'But the police . . .!' I try.

'The police can do whatever they like. They won't find a trace of Erica anywhere. They can go straight to Vigil HQ if they want but we'll never reveal squat about any of our own people. National security and all that. Erica is with me. She's fine. And she doesn't want to talk to you.'

'Wait!' I don't want him to hang up the phone just yet. There's too much I want to know. 'Can you at least pass on a message? Can you let her know that I'm still here?'

'Erica told me about your fight. Didn't you get the message? She doesn't want to be friends with you any more. She doesn't need you. Erica has bigger fish to fry right now.'

'Please, this is wrong. She has to at least talk to her mum. Please just tell her to come home.'

If I wasn't sure about Jay before, now I can say that I *really* don't like him. I'm sure Erica wouldn't do this if she wasn't being totally manipulated. What kind of Vigil is he? Never mind that – what kind of *person* keeps someone away from her friends and her mother?

But then I imagine Erica seeing my name come up on her phone and handing it over to Jay to handle. She can't even bear to speak to me. Maybe she's given up on her mother too.

Does that mean that I should give up on her? I've done what I can now, and Erica's made her feelings very clear, even if they are via Jay. I should go away and nurse my wounds, protect what's left of my pride. Except that I'm not sure that I could live with myself if I didn't carry on trying. And besides, what am I going to say to the police when they come knocking on my door? I still want to do something; even if I don't mean anything to Erica any more, she still means something to me.

It's nearly lunchtime so I go straight to the library instead of going back to class. Normally I would go and actually eat lunch first, but my appetite has deserted me. I just want to sit down and think for a moment about what I should do next.

I barely notice when Toby sits down across from me. He waves his hand in front of my face. We're not exactly back on speaking terms but I guess he senses that something is wrong and wants to help. I wish I was in the right kind of mood to appreciate it.

'Someone said you had to go to Mr Stanley?' he asks.

'Yeah...'

'What was that about?'

'Nothing...' I open up my science textbook and pretend to read.

'Was it to do with Erica going missing? Apparently her mum came into school and everything.'

For the briefest of moments I consider telling Toby everything, right there in the library. But I talk myself out of it before I even give the thought a real chance. Toby wouldn't be able to handle this kind of information; *I* can barely handle this information. And what's the point of bringing somebody else into this conspiracy who would only be as useless as me?

'Hey, Louise, are you OK?' I wish that he'd develop psychic powers and just understand everything without me having to say a word.

'No, not really,' I mumble before slumping forward on the desk.

'What's wrong?' He leans over too, so that our heads nearly meet in the middle of the table.

'I can't tell you.'

'You probably could though, if you really wanted to.'

I wish that was true.

'Have you heard about spider-goats?' Toby asks, and I turn my head so that I can give him an annoyed stare. 'I was reading about spider-goats. They're like these genetically modified goats that have spider glands in their udders, so that people can spin silk from their milk.'

'Why are you telling me this?' I moan.

'It was on a Vigil forum page I was looking at last night, because some people think that Vigil DNA is being used to develop new technologies and cures for diseases and stuff. Also, I was trying to make you smile a bit.'

'You were trying to make me smile by telling me about spider silk that can be pulled out from goats' udders?'

'At the very least I thought it might lead to a conversation or something.' He creeps a finger out and pokes me with it.

'Quit poking me,' I say.

'So quit being boring and miserable. Otherwise I'll have to start describing the specifics of genetically modified goat anatomy.'

We let the silence sit for a while, but it's not uncomfortable. I decide that I'd better get my pen out and at least look like I'm working, so that Mrs Fraser won't think I'm doing nothing and chuck me out.

'I meant what I said, you know,' Toby says quietly to me after a bit.

'About what? Telling me all about goats' udders?'

'No. About telling me stuff. You could probably tell me anything. If you wanted to, I mean.' He sounds nervous, and I'm at serious risk of blushing myself to death so I dare not look at him. He doesn't even know the effect he's having on me.

'You wouldn't understand, Tobes,' I reply.

'Is it girlie stuff?'

'No . . .' Cue further blushing. I lean my head right over my textbook and put my hand in front of my face so that he can't possibly see me.

'Then why can't you tell me?'

'Because there's every chance that your life might be at risk if I do? Plus I'm pretty sure that there'll be a ton of paperwork involved.'

He thinks I'm joking. When I don't say anything else he pulls out his own books and gets to work. After a few minutes I feel brave enough to take my hand away from my face and take a peek up at him. This is the most we've chatted in a while, without him bringing up my bunking off. But he thinks that a quick joke will make everything go away, as if my problems are normal and not weighed down by serious repercussions. God, I wish I had *normal* problems. If I'm in hot water, it's creeping up to my neck right now.

Then it hits me: what happens when you get yourself completely in over your head? You go and find a responsible adult to deal with the problem for you!

I just can't believe that Jay is following the proper procedure with regards to what's best for Erica, especially after what she's told me about how the Vigils work (even though that isn't a lot). Surely if I went to the Strand and spoke with the Vigil people themselves, they'd sort out this Jay mess and send Erica home before the police get too involved? Tomorrow is the weekend, and screw whatever homework needs doing; I'm going to take myself down to London and get this whole thing sorted out.

15

Saturday, and the garden is hidden under a sheet of frost. Everything looks so calm and serene. And yet the urge to act is striking me in the gut with electric bolts of energy. I can't even sit still while I eat my breakfast; my left leg is jumping under the table, the hand not holding my cereal spoon is tapping on the countertop. My heart races as I think about what I have to do today, and how I'm going to go about it. How exactly do you march up to the head-quarters of a superhero organisation and tell them you think that one of their members is up to no good?

I've been playing it out in my head and there's not a single scenario where I can imagine sounding remotely grown-up. And even in the best-case version, where the super-guys do their thing to find out what's been going on and reprimand Jay for being a colossal douche, how is Erica going to react afterwards? I mean, I'd like her to see the error of her ways, agree that Jay has been manipulating her all along and go back to being my friend, but what if she still absolutely hates me?

It's only when I'm putting the milk from my cereal away that I see the note my parents left me on the fridge. They've gone out early to an antiques fair out of town and won't be back until late afternoon. I suppose they thought I could use the quiet time to get on with revision. As if it's possible for me to focus on schoolwork right now.

While I shower I think about whether I'm just being a huge idiot about all of this. It's quite possible that Erica is absolutely fine, just getting on with her new life with her new superhero friends. There's every chance that I'd just be embarrassing her by getting involved and interfering in her dream, which would only make her hate me more. Maybe I should just stay at home today and think about making new friends, ones who appreciate good crochet skills and a mild stationery obsession.

My phone buzzes on my bedside table, and I groan, thinking that it's probably Toby asking me some stupid question about our physics homework. It may only be nine in the morning but I figure if anyone is going to be stuck into schoolwork at this time of day, it's going to be him.

Jay's coming after you! An unknown number.

The hairs on the back of my neck prick to attention.

Who is this? I type back, hesitating before I hit send.

It's Erica!!!!!!!!

I squeal and drop my phone, but rush to pick it up again and type back: *ARE YOU OK????? WHERE ARE YOU?????*

No time to explain! Get out of house and go somewhere safe! PLEASE!!!!

I hit the call button, hoping to get through to her right now and find out what the hell is going on. She's scaring me something silly, and yet there's also a bristling uncertainty that this could be a wind-up. I get straight through to an anonymous answer-machine service; the phone doesn't even ring.

PLEASE DON'T CALL. Another text message, just moments after I end the call without leaving a message. *YOU'RE NOT SAFE. GO HIDE BEFORE JAY FINDS YOU. PLEEEAASSSE!!!!*

I don't think I'll ever be able to forgive her if she *is* winding me up. I wish I knew what the hell was happening, but right now my gut is telling me to do exactly what she says and ask questions later.

I get dressed, quickly and haphazardly, wondering where Jay might be and how much time I have before he arrives. If he arrives. It hasn't left the realm of my imagination that this might all be some strange, elaborate bluff, or some weird punishment from Erica for what I said to her.

Once I'm bundled up in my duffel coat, bobble hat and scarf, I go into my parents' bedroom, which looks out on to the street. I peer through the net curtains, careful not to shift them in case anybody outside is looking for me. I'm just starting to think that whatever Erica's plan is, she's done a fantastic job of turning me into a paranoid freak, when I see a motorbike turn into my road. There's every chance that it's not Jay, that it's some other totally random person on a motorbike, but the heat in my ears and the pounding of my heart indicate that my paranoia was not misplaced. He's here. I need to get away.

When I get downstairs I twitch at the dining-room nets, peering out once again to check what's going on. He must have parked a little way down the road, as I can't see his bike from here. I can't hear it either. I can't leave my house by the front door. I'd be walking right up to him. I'll have to sneak out the back. I hurry into the kitchen and unlock the back door. Then just one more breath, and I'm gone.

Walking along the stepping stones set into our neat lawn, I'm acutely aware of the late November frost numbing my nose and the tips of my fingers, left bare by my fingerless mittens. At the bottom of the garden there's a loose fence plank that Dad was meant to fix years ago. When I was a lot younger I used to ease my way through it during games of hide-and-seek with my cousins, but now that I'm fifteen I find it almost impossible, despite my diminutive size. I have to take off my coat. I push it through the gap ahead of me and just about manage to squeeze myself through, quickly putting it back on once I'm safe on the other side.

What's Jay doing? Is he waiting at my front door after politely ringing the bell? Is he going to work out some way

169

to break in, thinking that I'm enjoying a lazy Saturday morning in bed?

I'm stuck behind some thick shrubbery, which is probably a good thing as I don't want my neighbours watching me hiding out in their garden while they eat their breakfast. I creep through the garden, edging slowly closer to the house. This whole time, I'm amazed at how measured and calm I'm acting. I'm putting it down to adrenaline. Something is pumping through me, keeping my breathing steady while my pulse races, getting me ready to run should I need to. It's exhilarating and terrifying all at once. I wonder if this compares at all to what Erica feels when she's doing her super-thing.

What I have to work out next is how to get myself out of this garden and onto the street. There's a gate to one side, but I can see a big padlock fixing it shut. Either I find my way through more back gardens until an opportunity presents itself, or I break into this house and go out their front door. Considering the fact that it's bright morning daylight, and the general niceness of people's fences around here, crawling through gardens won't be easy. But when I look towards the house along I notice a trellis with some dead plant climbing up it. It leads to their garage roof. Without thinking about what might happen next, I start to climb it like a ladder.

I'm actually on top of somebody's garage. I keep myself low, petrified that Jay has somehow realised that I've eluded him, and slink towards the edge. It's not that far a drop, not really. Only one storey. So why can't I move? I have to take a few more steadying breaths before I let my feet dangle over the edge, and then I hum to myself as I turn over, easing myself down so that I'm properly dangling, my cold fingers clinging and my arms shaking. Then I let go. The drop is measly, I know this, but I feel like I've scaled a pyramid or something. All that adrenaline jumps in my veins, forcing me to grin as I dart down the drive of this stranger's house and onto the street. I am basically a ninja.

Only once I'm certain nobody is following me do I dig out my phone and make the call. It's the only safe place I can think of.

'Hi, Toby – you home?'

'Yes...'

'Can I come over?'

'Do you know my address?'

'No. Can you give it to me?'

'Why? What's going on?'

'Can I tell you once I come over?'

'Maybe.'

'Seriously, Tobes.'

'It's a Saturday morning. What could possibly be so serious on a Saturday morning?'

'Toby!' And I have to yell it, even though I know that yelling makes absolutely no sense when trying to maintain

Ninja Stealth Mode. 'I'm in trouble, OK? I'm freezing and I just had to ninja stealth my way out of my own house, so will you please just give me your address?'

The silence from his end makes me think he's hung up on me, but it turns out he's thinking. Finally he relents and gives me his address, plus directions. He says it's a ten-minute walk, but I hurry and make it five.

Toby opens his front door but doesn't let me in straight away. I look round behind me, and fortunately there's no sign of any motorbikes following. Apparently I did it, and I'm free, for now.

'What's going on, Louise?' Toby asks while I'm freezing on his doorstep.

'Just let me in, OK?'

'You know you could just talk to me like a normal person, instead of being all dramatic.'

'Look, it's hard to explain, and I'm not entirely sure what I can tell you, but I needed somewhere safe to figure out what to do next.'

Toby makes a big gallant gesture of letting me in before leading me upstairs to his room. This gives me a few moments to ponder what exactly I'm going to tell him, and how I can get him to believe me. It's not as if we've been on the greatest of terms over the last few weeks, and I don't know what he must think of me for turning up like this. I realise that I could just make up something stupid like debt collectors arriving at my house when my parents are out, or that I'm having some sort of extreme panic attack over a piece of assessed work, but I don't want to lie. Not when I really need some help.

I might never have been round to his house before but I recognise Toby's room instantly. The door is entirely covered with fragments of posters and stickers, all linked to various levels of geekery. I recognise some gaming logos, bits of sci-fi jargon that's been scribbled over the tops of posters in Tipp-ex, plus some pictures of truly random things, like a purple jellyfish, and a banana with a smiley face. This door is a collage of Toby, and I love it.

His bedroom, meanwhile, looks like it's been struck by a Toby tornado. I can imagine his lanky arms flinging bits of clothing all over the place, so that a sock has ended up hanging over his desk lamp and instead of carpet or a rug, he has a pair of crinkled jeans strewn on the floor. Lined up under his bed, in an absurdly orderly fashion, is a collection of used glasses, mugs and plates, so many that I have to wonder what could possibly be left in the kitchen. Posters cover every plausible inch of wall space, and where a huge built-in cupboard takes over, the posters extend over that too. The ones that aren't all black and sci-fi are pictures of Vigils (mostly the female ones). Two clothes baskets are overflowing. I should probably mention the odour too. I can't quite pinpoint exactly what his room smells like, but it's definitely organic. A mixture of sweat and dead teabags, apple cores and deodorant spray. But the part of his room that appals me the most, and I can't help taking this quite personally, is the space reserved for his schoolbooks, which are littered all over the floor and the desk, all crumpled up and unloved. I heave a sigh of disappointment and fight the urge to put the books into a neat, organised pile.

'If you'd have given me more notice, I would have tidied up a bit,' Toby mumbles. I turn just in time to see him kick some underwear (dirty? Better not to know?) behind a chest of drawers. 'It's not usually this messy.' I don't believe him.

I see the shelf above his desk. Lined up perfectly straight, all facing forward, are these incredible Vigil models. They stand about fifteen centimetres high but vary in proportion with their real-life heights, so the Deep Blue figurine is slightly taller, the Red Rose one slightly shorter. They've each been expertly and perfectly painted. These aren't the usual kind of action figures you see in the toy shops, these are real collectibles, the types that I've seen advertised on Vigil fansites and are really expensive. And it appears that Toby has the full set. I can even imagine the Flamegirl – or is it Vega now? – figure standing right there between Quantum and Hayley Divine, and a wave of sadness, tinged with panic, washes through me.

How can I tell Toby what's going on without revealing the truth? Right here, in full view of his complete UK Vigil set (plus a few of the more popular American and

European Vigils, I notice), how am I meant to work out this elaborate lie?

So I give it my best.

'You're trying to tell me that Erica's psycho boyfriend has kidnapped her – *you think* – and is now after you? And you've come round to my place to hide? You do realise how ridiculous you sound, right?'

I have to agree; it sounds like the most stupid thing ever.

'Why exactly would he be after you?' Toby asks.

'I have no idea,' I reply, throwing my hands up in front of me in frustration.

'And what kind of person kidnaps their girlfriend? Louise, tell me the truth here, are you high?'

I sit down on Toby's bed (it's only half-made, so I sit on the made part) and I try not to think about the fact that I'm on Toby's bed. My friend Toby, who I might possibly like more than I really want to admit and who would never fancy me back because I'm just a boring girl who looks the complete opposite of all the girls whose pictures he's got on his walls. I wish I could be here under different circumstances, but the more I look around his room and at his Vigil figurines, the more I feel that I have absolutely no hope of getting him to see me as anything other than his library chum. And now a library chum who might also be sounding like a hysterical lunatic.

'You know yesterday in the library? When I was really upset?' I start, trying again to explain everything without revealing anything.

'Yup...'

'Well, I had just tried calling Erica, and Jay answered. And he was weird. Like, really weird. He told me that Erica couldn't come to the phone, and that she didn't want to talk to me. And just before that I saw Mr Stanley and Erica's mum, and they've called the police about her going missing. I think something is seriously wrong, and at first I was all like *Well, maybe I should just stay out of it*, because we've been fighting, but then this morning Erica gets in touch by text, from an unknown number, and she tells me to run away and hide because Jay is coming after me.'

'So what are you thinking? Isn't Jay her boyfriend? I mean, sure it's a little messed up if they've run away together, but why the hell would he be coming after you?'

'I'm serious about this.' I implore him with my eyes. I know that I'm still not making very much sense and that he's getting irritated.

Toby comes and sits next to me. I suck in my breath. Toby, right here, so close to me, in jeans and a ratty T-shirt, on his bed. He hasn't even sorted out his hair yet, and it sticks up at goofy angles that I just want to touch and tame. He nudges me with his shoulder, like he's trying to topple me over.

'I think you might be a little stressed out by exams. Do *you* think that you might be a little stressed out by exams?' he asks.

'Toby. I don't know any other way to explain it to you. Something is seriously wrong and Erica is in trouble. And...' I stop what I'm saying and think. 'And I need to go into London.'

'No. What you *need* to do is have a cup of tea, and then go home and get on with your revision,' Toby corrects.

'My plan was to go into town and get in touch with Jay's...' What do I call them? 'Jay's bosses. I know where he works, and if I could just get in touch with them, then maybe they can sort all of this out.'

'Louise...'

'You don't have to come with me. I just need to get to the tube station without Jay seeing me, and then everything will be fine.' Except that I don't want to move from where I am right now, from where it's safe and where Toby is.

'Louise...you should stay here for a bit. We have the same assignment in maths, don't we? We'll work on home-work together so that you don't get stressed out, and *then* everything will be fine.'

I get up to peek out of the window. Toby's tiny boxroom looks out on to the street below, and so far, no motorbikes in sight. Just a world starting to come to life on a Saturday morning: an old lady pushing a checked trolley on wheels out in front of her, and a couple of kids kicking a football against a garage wall.

'I really have to go,' I say, looking back around at a bewildered Toby.

'At least stay for a cup of tea? You'll feel better after that, I promise.'

I agree, but only because I feel that a cup of tea will be the perfect thing to brace me for going back outside. Plus I need to formulate the best route to the tube station, one that keeps me away from the main roads, where Jay might be prowling. While Toby makes the tea I roam his living room, dwelling on the collection of family photos on the mantelpiece. There's a couple of him and his older brother who went to university last year, plus a bunch of pictures of people I presume to be his grandparents. Toby's parents look nice. They're both tall, like him, but it's clear that Toby takes after his dad the most. They have the same dark hair and oversized features on lanky limbs, except that his dad has obviously grown into himself and looks strong and friendly.

'Where's your mum and dad?' I call into the kitchen as my eyes fall on pictures of Toby from when he was younger. I can tell that it's him because his brother is always significantly taller.

'My dad was talking at some big symposium in Wales yesterday,' he calls back. 'And they decided to stay the weekend. Milk? Sugar?'

'Yes and yes, please!' I reply. 'They let you stay home alone?'

'Well, obviously they've raised exactly the type of teenager who organises a massive rave the moment his parents are out of the picture,' he jokes as he comes back into the living room holding two mugs of tea. 'Oh, please don't look at those!'

Once I have my cup, Toby reaches over and turns around the photos of him as a baby.

'What? You were cute back then!' I tease.

'I had a fat face,' Toby whines, blowing on his hot tea.

'Every baby has a fat face,' I reply, reaching over to turn the picture back round. Toby doesn't stop me.

'You seem a bit calmer now,' he says when we sit down on the sofa. 'Are you absolutely sure that you need to go into town to rescue Erica, or do you think that perhaps you should stay here for a bit, drink my exceptional tea and help me nail maths?'

I don't want to keep going on about how serious I am, so I just give him a look and hope that it works.

That kind of puts a halt to the conversation, which is fine because it means I can enjoy the tea. When I start getting cold, I wonder how appropriate it would be to ask Toby if I could borrow one of his hoodies.

'Are you shivering?' he asks, looking at me weirdly.

'It's just suddenly got really cold in here, hasn't it? Can't you feel it?'

'I suppose it has.' Toby gets up and goes to check the nearest radiator. 'That's odd – it's still on.'

I turn away and look out the window. Except that I can't see out. The glass has completely clouded over, scattering the light and turning everything an eerie blue. The panes are marked by a flurry of patterns, like they've been turned to crystal. I can see my breath in front of me.

Toby stalks forward, treading softly like he's scared the windows will break, and I don't say anything at first because I'm fascinated as well. But then I realise that it hasn't stopped getting colder. The temperature is descending so rapidly that my lips are sore and it hurts to blink.

'Toby, wait,' I warn as he reaches out a tentative finger to the glass. He pulls away instantly as though he's been burned, and where his finger was, I notice a tiny white mark. The mark spreads out like a wondrous snowflake until the entire bay window is rippled with white lines, each one sounding like snapping chocolate as it spreads.

And then everything shatters. Tiny glass shards fly out, shimmering like glitter. I cower, attempting to cover my face, but I'm breathing in frozen air, the cold settling and caking my lungs. I can just about hear Toby calling my name, but soon the sound of the ice blizzard drowns out everything else and my ears become blocked up with the cold. I can't open my eyes, can't move save to try and bundle up further. Everything happens so quickly there's no time to register what is going on, to try to find a way out. I'm certain that I am dying. I'm going to be frozen solid, then I'll shatter like the window, until there's nothing left of me but a pile of silver dust floating on the blizzard wind.

16

It's dark when I wake up, and I can't move. My hands are behind my back. There's a tightness in my chest that makes me want to gulp in the air. My right shoulder is desperately uncomfortable, twisted around at a bad angle, but I can't really move it. All I can do is shift and squirm and wait for the familiar, painless click that will release it, allowing me to relax. It doesn't come. As I attempt to wriggle my shoulders, I find that my hands are actually fastened, at another uncomfortable angle, with plastic bindings. The more I try to move them, the more the bindings dig into my wrists. As sensation awakens lower down, I attempt to shuffle my legs, but they're under me and tied at the ankles. I cringe with pins and needles.

I can't tell where I am. My eyes haven't yet adjusted to the dark, and my panicked breathing stops me from concentrating. All my energy is focused on wriggling my fingers free or pulling at my legs, both apparently impossible.

Just shy of completely freaking out, I decide to slow myself down and attempt to regain some control. I close my eyes again, work at smoothing out my breathing, and try to relax my muscles so that the bindings at my ankles and wrists won't be quite so painful. It works, but then I open my eyes back into the darkness and I start to panic again. It's like sitting inside a black hole. I can feel my feet, and that I'm leaning against a wall and have been placed on something soft like a mattress, but there's an empty chasm that stretches all the way around me. I feel hopeless, like I might have been buried alive and forgotten about.

Something makes a muffled grunting noise behind me, but I can't twist round to see what it is. The grunting comes again, this time sounding like a tired moan. I know that sound: it's the sound Toby makes when Mrs Fraser presents him with a massive stack of books to shelve five minutes before the end-of-lunch bell rings.

'Toby?' I whisper. He must be right behind, bound and propped up on the mattress just like me. I try to shuffle backwards so that I can poke him.

'Too early, Mum...' he mumbles in response, clearly still asleep. 'Just a few more minutes, please...'

I'm slowly starting to realise that we're not in a pitch-black void. There's a window on one side of the room, and even though it's been blacked out with a heavy blind or curtain, there's a tiny aura of light that just peeks through, creating a frame in the darkness.

I try to remember exactly what happened when the window shattered, and how we could have possibly ended up here, wherever 'here' is. It must have been Jay, but he couldn't have caused all that snow and ice with his powers alone. He must have friends. And what's with the sleeping thing? Did he drug us?

'Toby!' I try again.

'Louise?' he mumbles back at me.

'Wake up!' I hiss.

I can tell that he's shifting on the mattress, trying to get comfortable.

'I'm tied up!' Toby says as he gains awareness.

'I know. I am too,' I tell him.

'Am I blind?'

'No...it's just really dark in here. Are you OK? Is anything hurt?'

'No, I don't think so. What about you?'

'I think I'm OK. We must have been knocked out somehow, or drugged. I have no idea where we are.'

'What the hell's going on, Louise? What is all of this?'

I'm struggling to think of a way to explain this other than with the truth, but after so many years of training myself into keeping secrets, it's not easy to let everything go just like that.

'I told you that I thought Jay was a bad guy...' is all I can think to say.

There's more movement, kind of like Toby's bouncing around behind me.

'What are you doing?' I hiss, scared that I'm going to

184

tumble over onto my side and won't be able to get back up again.

'Trying to escape,' Toby replies, although what I really think he's doing is causing a whole lot of commotion for nothing.

He shuffles, and I can imagine him contorting himself with his hands and ankles bound. There's a tumble and an audible 'Ooof' as he crashes to the floor. By the sound of it, it's a hard one.

'Are you all right?' I ask.

'Yes. Maybe . . . probably not,' he moans from his new position.

I think the racket Toby's making has alerted our captors. A door creaks and opens, the light slicing through the darkness. Now I can see we're in a bedroom. Stark, but also somehow messy, as if someone's just moved in and hasn't unpacked their stuff yet. Toby's on the floor on his back, but he's worked his hands out in front of him and is already starting to pick at the bindings on his ankle.

'Greetings and salutations!' Jay comes into the room and flicks on the light switch, casting the whole room in a glare that hurts my unadjusted eyes.

'Jay! What's going on? Where's Erica?' I ask, twisting myself round on the bed so that I can face him.

'Now, Louise, is that a nice way to talk to your host? You are guests here at my pleasure, so be nice.' He swans into the room, still wearing that wretched black trench coat, his hair oiled back away from his face. 'Now, let me introduce you to my friends, as I don't think you've been properly acquainted yet.'

Two more people come into the tiny bedroom. One of them looks like an American hip-hop gangster, complete with gold chains and a red bandana wrapped around his head. He looks a bit like a cartoon character, or like someone who has chosen a rapper as their fancy-dress inspiration. Except that he doesn't look amused by his choice of dress. He's sullen and angry, and I can imagine tense little eyes behind his dark sunglasses. The other one is a woman, tall and slim and wearing far too much blue eyeshadow. Her hair is cut pixie-short and is bleached brilliant white, and she has about ten different piercings in each ear, plus another one in her nose.

'Louise, Toby, please meet my good friends Dozer and Blizz.'

'Are they Vigils too?' I ask, which for some reason makes them all laugh hysterically, like I've just said the funniest thing in the world. Toby turns abruptly to look at me with an expression on his face that says, *WHAT?!?!?!*

'No, sweetheart, we are not the Vigils.' The woman, Blizz, has an Eastern European accent.

'I get to meet lots of fine folk on my travels scouting for new recruits,' Jay explains. 'Sometimes I come across young people like Erica, who are perfect for the club, and sometimes –' he pauses – 'I find others who are less suited.'

I glance towards Toby, whose face is a mix of elated fascination and terror. I can only imagine what he's thinking right now.

'So what's going on? Why have you kidnapped us?' I ask, surprised at the bravery in my own voice.

'Well, Louise, seeing as you were so desperate to be *involved* with everything earlier, I thought it was about time that we let you in. Turns out that you might be of use to us after all. So just sit tight and relax. We're going out to get some supplies, but we'll be back later. Dozer here will keep you company.'

Jay makes that face, a smirk that might otherwise look cute and mischievous, but now just looks strange and sadistic. The white-haired woman, Blizz, follows him out of the room, leaving us with the gangster rapper.

'Is Dozer your codename?' I ask him.

'Louise . . .' Toby hisses at me, wanting me to shut up, but I'm determined to figure out what exactly is happening, and this Dozer guy might be able to provide some answers.

'I ain't saying nothin' to you,' he replies. 'I'm just here to make sure you stay sweet and quiet. Ya hear me?'

'We hear you!' Toby says quickly before giving me another angry look.

'Just tell us what your power is, and then I'll be quiet.'

'You already seen it. Put you to sleep like you a baby.'

'You put us to sleep?' Toby says, stunned. 'Like, you knocked us out?'

'Nah, man. Gotta look me in the eyes, innit.'

'*Oh*, so you're Dozer like dozing off to sleep? That's a pretty neat name,' I say.

'S'all right.' He pauses to think. 'I'm gonna close this door now. Don't be doing nothin' stupid.'

The door closes, then locks, and Toby scoots round on his bum so that he's looking at me. I suppose now is the time for explaining everything then. He stares at me expectantly.

'So there's something I haven't told you . . .' I start.

'Ya think?' Toby sighs.

'So you remember Flamegirl?' I look at him. Of course he remembers Flamegirl. 'Well, turns out that she's actually Erica.'

'*Our* Erica?'

'Yup. Erica Elland is Flamegirl. And Jay was inducting her into the Vigils, except something has gone really wrong and I don't quite understand it and now we're caught up in it too.' Toby just continues staring at me. 'So now you know.'

I think his eyes are about to bulge out of his head. 'You're kidding me?'

'Nope. Definitely not kidding you. Definitely tied up right now by the bad guy.'

'No, but seriously, you're really not kidding me?'

'Toby!'

'Right. OK then.' He stares at the floor. I can practically see the cogs of his brain turning, processing this new and unbelievable information. Then he turns back to me. 'Is that Jay guy going to kill us?'

'Hopefully not?' I offer.

'So Jay goes around recruiting new Vigils? Is that what he said he does? And sometimes he finds people that aren't suitable, which I suppose makes sense, because not everybody who has superpowers has to be a good guy, I guess . . . So is he trying to put together a troupe of anti-Vigils? Hey, he could call them the *Vigil-Antis!*'

'Do you think he might have been trying to get Erica onside?' I ask, tactfully ignoring his joke, because really this is no time for puns.

'Well, I think you could be right about Erica being in trouble,' Toby concedes. He suddenly seems remarkably OK about everything, and I wonder if he's just putting on a brave face but is actually totally freaking out on the inside.

'But what does he want? What's he doing?'

I slump back against the wall. I'm so uncomfortable from having my hands tied up behind my back. Especially as I have an itch on my nose. I try to snub it out on my shoulder, but I can't quite get at it. Then I notice Toby moving awkwardly, jerking about on the wooden floor like he might be having a fit.

189

'Er . . . What are you doing?' I ask.

'Just trying to get something . . .' He scoots and slides and contorts his arms until finally he can reach inside the pocket of his jeans. Carefully he eases out a Swiss Army knife.

'What the hell?' I start, amazed.

'Shh!' he hisses. 'I was going to be working on another one of my Vigil models today, and sometimes there's some delicate work that needs doing, so I had it handy. Now keep quiet, otherwise Mr Dozey outside will hear us!'

Toby fiddles until he has the knife within his hands, and then fiddles around even more until he has the main blade out. Then he shuffles forward on his knees until he's sitting right in front of me. I turn my back to him and hold my bound hands out and slowly, carefully, he cuts at the plastic.

'You are a genius,' I whisper as finally my hands are free.

I quickly take the pocket knife from Toby and cut all of his binds free before he returns the favour by releasing my legs. I feel as if I've been holding my breath this entire time and it's only now that my lungs can work properly. Toby hides the knife back in his pocket; we both agree that we should keep its existence a secret for as long as possible.

'Right, so, next job involves unlocking the door. But what are we going to do about Dozey?' Toby says as we stretch out our arms and legs, shaking off the tension.

'Is there anything in here we can hit him with?' I ask, looking around the room.

'We can't actually hurt him, can we?'

'Hey,' I ponder. 'I wonder what happens when he looks in a mirror. Do you think he sends himself to sleep?'

'Or maybe he's like Medusa, and the only way we can look at him without turning to stone – or falling asleep, in this case – is by looking at his reflection.'

I glance around the room and see a small vanity mirror on the desk. It might be what we need to get out of here. I can hold it up in front of me like a shield the moment Dozer tries to put me to sleep. I don't know how his power works exactly, but it doesn't seem like a better plan is going to come along any time soon.

As I look more closely around the room, I come to the realisation that this must be Jay's bedroom, and the vanity mirror is what he uses to fix his hair in the morning. My first thought is *Ewww*, because I've been sitting on this creep's bed and I'm trapped in here, and somehow that thought has a weird potency. But when I look around properly I realise how sad Jay's life must be. There's the desk in the corner, above which are tacked various doodles and sketches, all in the same deep-blue ink. I guess he must have created them with his photocopying powers. But other than that, there's basically no decoration. Most of his stuff is piled in crates and boxes, and there's very little inside his wardrobe. Even the light bulb above us is bare.

'So if you get to do the mirror thing, then I totally get to do the door thing,' Toby says, reaching back into his pocket for the penknife.

'Are you going to actually pick the lock like a burglar?' I ask, incredulous.

'You have another idea?'

'It's not that I doubt the validity of the plan, I just doubt your ability as a burglar. Have you ever picked a lock before?'

'No. But I have watched a ridiculous amount of films and television. And that can't *all* be made-up, right? I've seen it done so many times. It can't be that hard.' He kneels down in front of the lock and fiddles about with various blades of the knife. 'There doesn't happen to be a paperclip on that desk anywhere, does there?'

I hand him a paperclip I find in the top drawer of the desk. It's a disorganised mess of a man drawer, crammed with receipts and AA batteries, pens and, bizarrely, a digestive biscuit. As Toby continues fiddling, his brow set with concentration, I search through the other drawers to see if there's anything else I can use for our daring escape. I don't know what good a USB cable or a roll of gaffer tape will do, but I stuff them in my pocket anyway.

There's an audible click and I realise that Toby's obsessive box-set binging has paid off. I watch him turn the handle and then slowly ease the door open.

'Do you have the mirror?' he whispers.

I do. I creep out in front of him, holding the mirror out in front.

From the corridor we can hear the TV on in the front room, and Dozer chatting, presumably on the phone, in his gangster slang. Imagining that I'm as brave as Theseus, with wings on my shoes to lighten my steps on the creaking floorboards, I edge forward, tilting the mirror so that I can see around the corner. Toby creeps behind me, and even though I can't see him, I can sense his panic.

There's Dozer. He's lounging on the sofa, legs sprawled out in front and chatting into a phone while the TV blares. I guess that's why he hasn't heard us. All I have to do is catch him off-guard, get in his line of sight and reflect his power when he tries to use it on me. Easy, right? There's sweat on my temples and I'm biting my lips. I feel as if my ninja skills have deserted me.

I creep, until finally I know I have to lunge.

That thing they say about everything going so fast it's a blur? Well, it's just like that. I'm moving forward and he's jumping up, and then instead of my fabulous reflecting plan happening, I instinctively go to use the mirror like a bat, reaching around to hit him and hoping that I can knock him back. I'm thinking that I'm an idiot, and what kind of ridiculous little girl attempts to do something this audacious to a man nearly triple her size, when I sense something moving behind me. Then suddenly there's a vase, complete with flowers, crashing down on Dozer's head, sending him thundering to the floor.

'Oh my God, what happened?' I ask. Even though my hands are shaking, I can't let go of the mirror.

'I saw a vase . . .' Toby says, out of breath and obviously a little bit in shock himself. 'I just went for it!'

Dozer is completely out. On a nearby coffee table I see a bag stuffed with the same kind of plastic ties that were used on me and Toby, so we use them to secure the big guy to the radiator. We replace his sunglasses, then use the gaffer tape and gag him in case he wakes and can use his voice to send us to sleep too. We pause over our handiwork, still breathing hard and shaking, but all in all, it's a job well done.

'Now what?' Toby asks.

'We need to get to Vigil headquarters and tell them what's going on,' I say.

'Great. First, though, I need the loo.'

Toby disappears and I survey the scene. I'm a little bit annoyed by the soil and bits of flower and plant that are all over the floor (it seems so unnecessarily messy), but I'll just have to get over it.

'Erm . . . Louise?' Toby calls from down the corridor. 'You'd better get down here.'

I roll my eyes. I'm really not in the mood for one of Toby's silly toilet jokes, but I decide to go and investigate because I figure that he probably isn't in the mood for one of his jokes either. He's standing in the doorway to the bathroom, staring at something with disbelief. I assume that it must be a spider or something, another thing I'm really not in the mood for, but when I can see in, I share his shock.

It's Erica.

17

She's frozen solid like a statue. She's standing upright in the bathtub, propped against the tiled wall, looking unharmed but ice cold and still. My fingers slide over the slippery leather-like material of her suit. On her blue-tinged face is a perfect frozen tear, a tiny polished crystal on her cheek. Her defensive stance, legs ready to run and palms out, heightens the uncanny spectacle. I touch my own palm to hers, but quickly remove it. The cold burns.

'Is she dead?' Toby stutters, still standing back in the bathroom doorway.

'I don't know,' I mutter, eyes fixed on Erica as I try to contain my shock and fear. Could she be dead? Or is this just some kind of freaky superhero magic? 'I know that she heals pretty fast, but what if she's too cold? This must be what that Blizz lady can do. She freezes stuff, like your windows earlier. She must have frozen Erica solid.'

'Should we try to defrost her?' he asks.

I reach up to touch Erica's hair, but back off again, fearing it might crack and shatter under my touch. Her eyes are open, which is the most painful thing, because she looks terrified. How could she have let this happen? She can't have been like this for long; she only texted me this morning. Maybe Jay found out that she had been in touch and this was her punishment.

'Can you go and fill up a kettle?' I say to Toby, Sensible Mode overriding my panic as I turn on the hot tap and realise that it's running cold. 'Maybe see if you can find the boiler and check that it's on? We need lots of hot water. And I'm going to see if I can find a hairdryer or something.'

Toby goes off to the kitchen, which frankly is a bit more like a large cupboard in this horrible little flat, and I go back into the room where we were held captive, hoping that Jay's vanity and reliance on hair products means that he'll have a hairdryer. He does. It's old and the fan at the back is all furred up, but after I plug it in I'm relieved to see that it still works. I'm pleased to see that there's a plug socket right outside the bathroom door, but when I stretch the cord I realise that it's not going to reach far enough. If I can shuffle Erica along to the other end of the bath, the end nearest the door, then maybe it will.

'What are you doing?' Toby asks, finding me attempting to reach under Erica's arms and drag her, trying not to smack her too hard against the bathroom tiles.

'The hairdryer won't reach,' I reply, before he comes over to help me.

I can tell that he's not comfortable with touching Erica and doesn't know where to place his hands, but otherwise I'm really surprised at how well he's dealing with the situation. Who'd have suspected Toby would be good in an emergency?

'I'm really sorry about all of this,' I say as we carefully hobble a rigid Erica along inside the tub like a shop mannequin, then lean her back up against the wall.

'Yeah . . . well . . .' Toby says.

'You're not freaking out or anything.'

'Oh, trust me, freaking out is going to happen. I'm just saving it all for later.'

'You could go, you know,' I say, pausing to rub my hands together to get rid of the biting cold from touching Erica. 'You could get out of here right now and save yourself.'

'And leave you here? Never going to happen.'

He looks at me, a look so determined and sincere that it makes my heart flutter. And then I have to tell myself off, because I'm pretty sure that it's not at all appropriate to have heart flutters when you're defrosting your frozen-solid best friend. I need to be focused, and I need to save Erica. Except, now that I'm looking at Toby under the harsh bathroom lighting, I think that he might be blushing. It could be because of his proximity to Flamegirl, or it could be because of me. It's the not knowing which that makes my heart beat even faster.

'You should go and check on the kettle,' I say when things start to feel a little too awkward.

When he comes back we both just stand there for a minute, wondering how the hell we're going to tackle this.

'We should start with her head, right?' I ask Toby.

'I have absolutely no idea. I wouldn't even know how to defrost a chicken.'

'Well, we can't burn her, that I do know. She's impervious to that. But I don't know if the cold might be harming her somehow. How long should it take to thaw a human being?'

'Again, absolutely no idea.'

I decide that we should start with her hair, and then work downwards from her head to her toes. Toby handles the kettle and slowly lets it pour over Erica. I then run over her with a towel, making sure that the hot water has permeated the whole way through. When the kettle is empty, I send him out to boil it up again, while I use more towels to mop up. Even though we are apparently able to defrost her skin, I worry that the cold goes a lot deeper than that. After three runs of the kettle and constant checking of the hot tap, which is still running cold, she's still too frigid to move, so I start to attack her with the hairdryer, searching her face for any sign that she might be conscious or able to hear us. Toby continues pouring boiling water over the back of her suit, using towels like flannels to dampen some of the harder to reach places, while I fire at her with the hairdryer like it's a ray gun.

And then she blinks.

I think it's a mirage at first, but when she does it again I know that it's real. She's alive!

'Erica? Can you hear me?' I ask, shaking her. She blinks frantically. 'Toby! Quick! Help me lie her down!'

She's now just about pliable enough to manoeuvre into the recovery position. We rest her down in the tub, which we've lined with more towels to make it soft and comfortable, and I angle the hairdryer, its cable stretched completely taut, so that I can keep on blasting her face with heat. Toby disappears to fill up the kettle once more, and I'm relieved to find that when I check the bath tap again, the water is beginning to run hot. I soak a towel and use it like a large flannel to apply hot pressure to her body. There's definitely some life back in her face. Although her lips and around her eyes are still rather blue, the muscles around her mouth have thawed and there's an expression there. One of pain and exhaustion.

'Hey, Erica.' I kneel and stare her straight in the eyes, talking over the blast of the hairdryer. She stares back with burning intensity. 'You've got to do your heat thing, OK? We're working really hard to thaw you out, but you've got to work too. Just think of all the amazing things, like flying and flame-throwing, and explosions and stuff. Can you do that?'

She just about manages a nod, then closes her eyes in concentration. I grip her hand, even though it's uncomfortably cold for me, and will some of my own body heat into her. I try to feel it, try to feel that warmth I'm used to, but it's not there. She's still too cold.

'Louise,' Erica says through chattering teeth.

'Erica! Please, please warm up!'

'What are you doing here?' I can only just about make out what she's saying, her jaw is shivering so much.

'Jay kidnapped us. Toby is here too; he's helping. We managed to get free, and then we found you. Please hurry up and get warm so that we can get out of here, *please*.'

'Toby?' Erica stutters.

'Er...hi, Erica,' Toby says, bashful as he gently pours more boiling water over Erica's legs. 'Sorry about this. And in case you were conscious before, sorry about possibly touching your...you know. It was completely accidental.'

Erica laughs. It's not an easy laugh, and it doesn't look comfortable, but it shakes her shoulders and makes the shivering subside for a moment. She looks like she wants to cough as well, but I don't think her chest is thawed enough for her to do that yet. I press a towel down on where her heart is, hoping that the wet warmth seeps deep into her.

'Keep talking, make her laugh,' Toby urges, before he leaves to fill up the kettle once more.

'Erica,' I start, 'remember when we first realised you could fly?'

'Hey! No cool stories before I get back in there!' Toby calls out from the kitchen.

'Don't worry about Toby,' I whisper to Erica, my face close to hers. 'I was really worried about telling him, and I tried not to for as long as possible. But there comes a point when you're both kidnapped and tied up by crazy people with superpowers where you just have to tell the truth. And he's being really cool about it. I thought he'd go totally fanboy crazy or something, but to be honest, I think I'd be having a complete nervous breakdown if he wasn't here with me. Plus I'd never have escaped by myself.'

'It's cool,' Erica manages to mutter. 'Are you all right?'

'I'm fine, we're both fine. We have that guy Dozer knocked out and tied up in the living room, and I guess that Jay will be back here pretty soon, but what we really need is for you to defrost and get your strength back so that we can get ourselves out of here.'

'I'm sorry...'

'Don't be sorry.' I think I might start crying. 'We'll talk about everything later. Right now, just get yourself warmed up.'

'OK, I'm back!' Toby reaches over the bath with the kettle and starts work on Erica's legs. 'Now tell me all your awesome superhero stories, please!'

I look from Toby's face, eager and alert and desperate to help, down to Erica's, with her eyes closed, lips still trembling from the cold. I'm worried that we're not working quickly enough.

'So you were staying over at my house,' I start, praying that telling this story will coax some life and energy into her, 'and I woke up sweating, with my pyjamas sticking to my skin. It was so hot you would have thought that it was the height of summer, but it wasn't. It was February – last year – and it was freezing outside. It was two in the morning, and I knew that it must have been you causing the heat, but you hadn't had a flush like that in ages. I was scared that you'd set fire to my bedroom. Mum had set up the camp bed and positioned it at the end of mine, but it was quite low so I shouldn't have been able to see you. Nonetheless, there you were, lying down and fast asleep, right in my eye line. I rubbed my eyes. I thought I might still be asleep and dreaming, or that I had confused some shadows because it was dark. But I went closer, and finally realised that you were *levitating*. I thought you were possessed, because you were obsessed with horror films at the time and had made me watch loads of them with you. I couldn't believe it.'

'You were flying in your sleep?' Toby asks, eyes and mouth agog with wonder.

'I had no idea I was doing it,' Erica mumbles, clarifying.

'I didn't know whether I should wake you up,' I continue. 'I wanted to, but it might have caused you harm, like how you're not meant to wake up sleepwalkers. Besides which, the closer I got, the more I was blasted by that heat. Finally I worked up the resolve to get close enough to touch you, but you were too hot. I could barely poke you without burning myself. So I found a knitting needle and poked you until you yelped and crashed back down on the bed. I told you that you'd been flying, and you didn't believe me, even though you had been dreaming about it for ages. And then you wouldn't go back to sleep because you were so desperate to try the flying out. You wanted to sneak out of my house and go down to the park right there and then, but I wouldn't let you.'

'So when did you actually figure out how to make the flying work?' Toby asks.

'You weren't there for that,' Erica tells me. I try to get her to hush, but it's obvious that she wants to tell the rest of the story herself. 'Every time we tried to make the flying happen, it wouldn't. Like the more we tried, the more impossible it seemed. And then one day, like a completely shallow doofus, I tripped while checking my reflection in a shop window.'

'You admit you were looking now?' I turn to Toby. 'She used to swear that she wasn't being vain!'

'Whatever. I'm over it. I tripped and was about to land flat on my face, when I just stopped. And I could feel it in my tummy, this pressure that was holding me just inches from the ground, and I knew I could do it.'

'But then she had to actually let herself fall, so nobody would know that anything strange or unusual was going on,' I finish.

We laugh, the three of us, and for a moment it feels easy, like this is totally how things are meant to be and Toby was involved all along.

'So how long have you guys been looking after each other? With all the superpower stuff, I mean?' Toby asks. He sees us exchange a look and quickly adds, 'You don't have to tell me. You really don't. I mean, you must have been keeping the secret for ages and I don't expect to be automatically included, even though I basically am now, but still.'

'It's OK,' Erica says, her voice clearer now that her breathing is easier. 'I mean, I'll kill you with my bare flaming hands if you tell anyone, but it's OK, really.'

'How about we fill you in on everything later?' I say to Toby. He nods in agreement before I turn back to Erica. 'How are you feeling?'

'I can feel my feet and wiggle my toes,' she replies.

'Do you think you could get out of the bath? I think moving around would really help,' Toby suggests. I feel this strange gush of pride that he's my friend and he's being so cool with all of this.

Each of us taking one of her freshly thawed hands, we ease Erica out of the tub. She doesn't seem to quite be able to support her own weight, so Toby and I each wrap an arm around her and help her to Jay's bedroom. We wrap her up in his duvet and then sit with her, waiting for her to let us know when she's ready to move. I hope it's soon. I just want to get out of this place as quickly as possible.

'How are you feeling now?' I ask her.

'Better. Just...so cold. I can't remember the last time I felt cold,' Erica admits. 'It's Blizz. Short for Blizzard. She's basically a snow queen. Also, she hates me. God, I can't believe she actually froze me. She *froze* me!'

'Couldn't you stop her?' Toby asks.

'It was a surprise. I wasn't expecting it. One minute I was arguing with Jay – about Louise actually – and then the next minute she'd come up behind me and had her hand on my shoulder and then everything went cold and dark. Oh my God – Jay. Where is he? What's he doing?'

'He went out with Blizz,' I explain. 'Erica, what the hell is going on with him?'

'He's a total psycho.' Erica sighs. Then she turns directly to me and clasps my hands in hers. 'I'm so, *so* sorry about him. I honestly had no idea. He's meant to be one of them, except what I think was happening was that he was just grooming me for his master plan.'

'And what is that exactly?' I ask.

'He wants a revolution. He wants the Vigils to forsake money and fame and glory-hunting and return everything to how it was years ago. Which sounds OK, except that he also hates everything about them. He's really angry, and I think he wanted to use me like a bomb or something.'

'A *bomb*?' I think about what Erica told me before, about Jay calling her his *little bombshell*.

'He thought he could convince me to go into the Strand and use my powers to blow the place up. Literally destroy everything there with my powers so that the London team would have to start all over again. When I went away last week I was so angry, and he seemed to be the only person who was listening to me, so I went along with his ideas. But then he started getting really weird, and I realised that instead of just *talking* about his crazy plan, that he was actually going to go through with it. I played along for a bit because I had no idea what else I was meant to do – he was starting to get scary – but then yesterday, when you called and he wouldn't let me speak to you, it got even weirder. This morning, when I texted you, that's what we were arguing about. He'd been trying to convince me to join his little gang, and then he went crazy when I finally stood up to him and said no. I can't believe Blizz froze me solid to keep me here!'

'It's OK, we've got you now,' I reassure her. 'We'll get out of here and we'll go find the real Vigils and they'll stop Jay. He hasn't got a plan if he hasn't got you.'

'Do you think you're ready to walk yet?' Toby asks.

'Maybe.' Erica holds up one of her hands in front of her face, blotchy red with chilblains. She rubs her thumb and forefinger together, and I wait for the flame to come. It doesn't. 'Damn it,' she curses.

'It'll come back. You just need to warm up some more,' I say.

We hear a noise, and at first I presume it's just the sound of the pipes after our epic hot-water session, but Erica looks concerned.

'Is that Dozer?' she asks.

'We tied him up; he can't go anywhere,' Toby says. 'But I'll just go and check...'

'God, I just feel so stupid about everything. Louise, I'm so sorry about the things I said. So, so sorry,' Erica says once Toby has left.

'Relax, it's OK. We've been worried about you, and your mum is really worried, but we've found you now, and we'll get you home and then the Vigils can sort this whole mess out. It'll all be fine, don't worry.'

'I totally fell for it,' Erica admits. 'I thought he really liked me. When I think about how he managed to manipulate me, I'm just so embarrassed.'

At first I don't notice that Toby hasn't come back into the room. I'm so concerned with Erica, with keeping her warm (I'm rubbing her body over the duvet she has wrapped around her in an effort to get her blood pumping), that for the moment it's pretty easy to forget about him. She repeats how sorry she is, and I keep telling her that it's fine, until I realise how quiet the flat is.

'Where's Toby?' Erica asks, picking her head up when she notices I've tensed up.

'Shhh...' I hiss, nervous. When I don't hear anything, I call out his name. He doesn't reply.

'Could Dozer have got him?' Erica whispers to me.

Then I hear it: the tentative creak of a floorboard, and no Toby appears. Footsteps, approaching slowly down the landing, and another set coming up the stairs.

'Oh no,' Erica murmurs as Jay appears in the doorway.

I was expecting Jay to be angry. The fact that he's not only makes the situation more fraught. He glides into his bedroom, hands behind his back, almost smiling. I wonder if this serene state is just masking a volcano of emotions bubbling under the surface. Will he erupt? And what's going to set him off?

'Please, let us go. I'm not going to help you with your plan. If you just let us go now and forget about everything, then I won't tell anyone what's been going on. Things can just go back to normal, like nothing has happened,' Erica reasons.

'You think it's that easy to shut everything down? Things are in motion. Cogs are turning. The world is changing, and if you think I can just stop it, you are sorely mistaken,' Jay replies.

'Where's Toby?' I ask.

Jay indicates that we're to follow him into the other room. Erica shucks off the duvet that's wrapped around her and takes my hand in hers. I'm startled by the coolness of it.

Back in the living room, Dozer is positioned exactly as he was before: on the sofa, with his legs sprawled out in front of him, chuckling into his phone and using slang words I don't recognise. His eyes are hidden behind his wraparound sunglasses, which is a relief, but also kind of unnerving because I can't tell what he's looking at. Toby is slumped at his feet, completely out of it, a gentle snore the only indication that he's alive.

'Hey, boss, check it!' Dozer calls out, tilting his head towards Jay to indicate who he's talking to. 'It's all working out!'

He grabs the remote control next to him, and while apparently still holding his conversation on the phone, turns the volume of the television up.

It's one of the news channels, and in bold across the bottom of the screen is the breaking news: SCOTTISH NUCLEAR POWER PLANT IN CRISIS.

'What's going on?' Erica demands, one of her hands still holding mine. I begin to feel the first stirrings of heat within her. I don't let go. 'You weren't meant to hurt anybody!'

'Relax, it's not that bad,' Jay says.

'Not that *bad*? A nuclear meltdown?' Erica cries.

Blizz, who is sitting on one of the armchairs, sighs dramatically and rolls her eyes, like none of this matters and we're boring her. But I'm with Erica – a power-plant crisis seems like a pretty big deal, not something to take lightly.

'Do you know how many fail-safes there are to prevent an actual nuclear meltdown? It's practically impossible to cause any real damage. What we've done is trip a few wires, knock out the odd computer and make a few lights blink. And even if something did actually go dangerously wrong, the Vigils would be there in moments. A national crisis like this and they'll all be there, vying for the spotlight. As usual.'

'Leaving the Strand without any defence...' Erica mutters, realisation creeping in. She looks back up at Jay, 'You're still going to go through with the plan, even though I told you that I wouldn't be a part of it? You can't make me do something I don't want to.'

'Oh, can't I?' And suddenly Jay is by my side. He's wound his way between me and Erica and I lose her hand. He comes behind and wraps an arm around my neck, and if he had a knife I'd think that he was trying to reach around to hold it to my throat. Instead he swipes his thumb across my cheek. It's a move that makes me physically gag. It feels like he's trying to wipe his thumb clean on my face, but there's a slickness, like he's smeared something on me.

'Leave Louise alone,' Erica warns, her voice low.

I touch my fingers to my cheek, and when I bring them away again I find my fingers covered in wet blue stuff. He inked me! The bastard inked me! It's creepy and deeply disturbing, and when I realise how easily he could have got to my eyes, I shudder.

'Here's what is going to happen,' Jay says to Erica calmly. He's still standing behind me and clamping his hands down on my shoulders, keeping me in place when I try to squirm. 'You're going to do exactly what I tell you to do, because otherwise your friend here is going to be in deep trouble. So let's say you head down to the Strand now, swoop in and do that big explosion thing you've become so proud of, and when Blizz tells me the job has been done, your friends will be allowed to go home.'

'You're holding them hostage?'

'I'm just going to keep them safe and sound right here. What happens to them ultimately is all down to you. Go home now and forget this whole thing ever happened, and I can guarantee that you'll never see your friends again. Go through with the plan, and I'll have no need to hurt them. Easy-peasy, and all down to you.'

'Don't, Erica. Whatever it is he wants you to do, don't do it!' I say.

She looks straight at me, and then glances down at Toby, still asleep and oblivious. Her hands ball into tight fists, and maybe I'm imagining it, but I think I can see them emitting a faint heat shimmer. Her powers are starting to return.

'You promise me that the Scotland thing isn't a big deal?' Erica asks Jay. 'Because if I find out that you've been hurting more people, or putting lives at risk...'

213

'You don't think Quantum and his boys and girls can figure out how to solve a little technical glitch? Deep Blue solves crossword puzzles more complicated than this. We both know what's going to happen. They're all going to traipse to Scotland, there'll be cameras everywhere, and all those flyers are going to strike their poses next to the cooling towers. And most importantly, they'll be gone long enough for you to do your thing without anyone interfering.'

'What about all the regular people who work at the Strand? What about the other agents who'll be there?'

'We talked about this. You can set the fire alarm off first if you like. I don't care. All I want is for that bloody place to be wiped off the map by the end of the day. You do your job, and your friends get to go home and watch *EastEnders* with a nice mug of cocoa.' Jay's hands clamp down even harder on my shoulders, and I think about his inky slime going all over my top.

'Erica, you don't have to,' I say again.

She looks worried. 'He'll hurt you and Toby,' she replies. 'I have to go.'

She takes her mask from Blizz, who has reached behind her armchair to pull it out from where it was presumably left crumpled on the floor. Erica dusts it off first, before fixing it on her face and adjusting her hair so that it's out of the way, using her heat-charged fingers to comb through and dry any strands that are still wet from her defrost. It's the first time I've seen her wearing her full costume, and if it wasn't for the sad expression on her face, she'd look magnificent.

'Erica...' I start. I want to tell her to walk taller, to hold her shoulders back so that she looks prouder, but with Jay's hands still attached to *my* shoulders, keeping me in place and stopping me from bolting, it would be stupid.

'You'll look after them? You won't hurt them, and you'll let them go as soon as the job is done?' she asks.

'You have my word,' Jay replies, taking one hand off me and holding it to his heart.

'They won't question why I'm there?' Erica asks, putting off the moment when she has to say goodbye.

'You just walk up to the door and walk in like nothing is wrong. If anyone questions you, just tell them you're there for training. Nobody will worry about what the Vigils' newest, brightest young star is up to. This is what's so gloriously special about you, my dear: you're a bomb in sheep's clothing. You get yourself into position, sound off the alarm to get everybody else out of there, and then when I know that everything is in place, I'll give you the call. Just remember to wait for my call before you do your thing.'

'There must be another way,' I butt in, feeling desperate. 'Erica, you'll be throwing away everything you've been dreaming of!'

'Shut up,' Jay says, pushing both hands back down on me. 'Erica is part of the great new future, a future that's not reliant on corporate greed. She understands what this is about and knows that the message needs to be loud in order for it to be heard.'

'Don't worry about me,' Erica says to me. 'It'll be quick, and I'll be fine. Just look after yourself and Toby. Soon all of this will be over and we can go home, OK?'

I glance down at Toby, who's developing a drool glob that looks set to land on the carpet at any moment. I wonder if it isn't too much to ask to be put to sleep until this whole mess is over. I don't want to think of Erica doing anything that could cause trouble or hurt people. Erica doesn't want to do this either. Whatever Jay has planned, there must be a way around it.

Blizz gets up from her armchair and goes to open the window. It slides up with a jagged creak, and then she holds it there, waiting for Erica to come over and clamber out.

'I'm sorry about all of this,' Erica says, and just at that moment, when she's right by the window and has her hands on the ledge, I think that all she has to do is turn round and incinerate this room. One mega heat pulse would be all it would take to do away with Jay and his nasty little gang, but then I would be gone too. I'm Jay's human shield. She'd have to burn through me to get to him. And with Toby on a cheap-looking carpet that is no doubt synthetic and flammable, I guess she's already weighed up her options and decided that going along with

Jay's scheme is the best plan for everyone. Even if it means destroying everything she wants.

Before I can say anything else, any words of wisdom or encouragement or hope, she's gone, flying up and away into the distance, leaving me breathless, scared and feeling very alone.

Jay turns to Blizz. 'Use my bike. Get down there fast. If anything happens that isn't to plan, you find your way in there and sort it out. Call me if there are any problems. I'm not leaving anything to chance. Dozer, you take that cretin downstairs and load him into the car.'

'Where are you taking him?' I ask, frantic as Dozer gets up and reaches down to flip Toby over his shoulder.

'We're all going on a little trip,' Jay reveals.

'What? Where? You told Erica that we'd be here waiting for her!'

'I tell Erica a lot of things. But I'll tell *you* something: you are becoming a right pain in my arse.' He turns to Blizz, who's about to leave the room. 'One more thing, love, before you go.'

He reaches around me and draws my wrists together, holding them out towards Blizz, who glides back over to us with a wicked smile on her face. She takes over the hold, gripping me with surprisingly strong arms for someone so slender. Then comes the cold. It seeps out from Blizz's hands and flows into mine, and at first I panic because I think she's going to freeze me completely solid like she did to Erica. I watch as the cold settles into my wrists until I can't feel my hands any more. They just hang there, blue and limp and clasped together. She's cuffing me with ice, and very quickly I find that I'm locked into crystalline manacles.

She gives Jay a kiss on the lips with a disgustingly audible slurp, winks at him with those ice-cold eyes and departs.

'Where are we going?' I ask again, tugging at my hands to try to pull myself free. My icy cuffs are sharp and painful; I quickly have to give up. I can barely wiggle my fingers and the cold seeps through my blood right up to my elbows. This is going to get uncomfortable very quickly.

'We're taking a little jolly to the Strand. It's just not in me to keep you and your BFF apart.' Jay shoves me so that I move forward and down the stairs to the flat's entrance. Dozer, carrying Toby like he is nothing more than an oversized rag doll, follows behind us.

We pile into a small car, with Dozer at the wheel. Bizarrely, and in a turn that I can only put down to megalo-maniacal lunacy, Jay reaches around me to make sure that my seat belt is done up. He does the same with Toby, but not before slapping him around the face a bit to make sure that he's definitely still conked out.

'Leave him alone,' I urge through gritted teeth.

'I take road safety very seriously, I'll have you know,' Jay replies, smiling. 'We don't want anything to happen to you two along the way.'

'Why are you taking us to the Strand? What's going on?' I ask once Jay has settled into the front passenger seat next to Dozer. But instead of replying, he turns the radio on all the way up, blasting dark, heavy rock music that cuts through my ears like chainsaws. Miraculously, and perhaps blessedly, Toby remains completely asleep.

We're going to the Strand. I don't understand why this is necessary, except... But Jay wouldn't do that. He put his hand on his heart and promised Erica that we'd be safe as long as she followed through with his plan. He couldn't do that, could he? But it would solve the problem of making sure that we stayed quiet after the event. If we were gone, conveniently placed in the path of Erica's destruction, we'd perish as soon as Jay gave her the go-ahead.

Jay doesn't want to keep us safe. He wants to do away with us permanently. And he's going to arrange it so that Erica does the job herself.

'All my life, I wanted to be one of them. And it wasn't just about the superpowers either. It was everything. The fame, the glory; I wanted to show everyone who had ever put me down. I would show them all.'

Jay's turned the volume down on the music as we approach central London. He's talking and talking and I let him, because I have no idea what else I'm meant to do. I'm lost. Erica's gone, and Toby's sitting beside me, snoring soundly as if nothing could possibly be wrong.

'But you know what the reality is? You want to know what it's really all about for your precious Vigils? Money. Targets. Popularity. Everything's like one big contest to them; who can earn the most? Who looks best in photos? Who has the hottest outfit? I wanted to rescue Erica from all that before she got in too deep. She's better than that crap, but her corruption was inevitable. She would end up just like the rest of them, consumed by her own vanity and greed. You know how this whole show is going, right? What it's going to turn into eventually? Premiership football clubs signing up

Vigils to patrol stadiums on big match days, corporations hiring Vigils as spokespeople. Not so bad, but then, a factory burns down: well, no one will save the people there because the local Vigils are funded by a competitor. If the governments can't offer bribes, then there'll be nobody to save the victims of the next train wreck. If a plane crashes in the wrong postcode, then wave goodbye to any survivors.'

'That hasn't happened yet. And how does blowing up the London headquarters change anything?' I say, angling my head slightly so that I can see myself in the rear-view mirror, spying the ugly, war-paint streak of ink across my face.

'They need to wake up! They need to take a step back and realise that what they are doing and where they are heading is wrong! The message needs to go out that we won't stand for it! And who better to send the message than the newest, brightest young recruit? Revolutions don't begin with a whisper, they start with a bang.'

'There must be another way,' I say, almost to myself really. I'm certain that Jay would never really take the time to change his mind about all of this.

'I've been in that Vigil gutter too long. Imagine what it's like when you wake up to find out you have superpowers, and a whole world of glory is spread out before you, only to then discover you're not wanted. You're sub-par, barely magic enough to make it into the fanzines. The Vigils tell you that they can give you everything, and what happens?

I'm relegated to being the office errand boy, given the name *Copyboy*, like I'm some delinquent intern, and paid barely enough to live on, while the flyers and the ones with the model good looks get the sponsorship deals and the front pages. Do you know what it's like to think you have it all, only for *it all* to mean absolutely nothing? Well, now they're going to see. Now they're going to have to face up to the consequences of their greed and vanity. Let's see how they like it when they have no base for their operations.'

I think about this, about how if the London base didn't exist, the UK Vigils would have to go to the next nearest base, maybe Paris or Barcelona, leaving the UK wide open. If a major disaster happened, if the Scotland power plant was a real and serious crisis, would they be able to get there in time?

We're nearly there. The car curls around Trafalgar Square before turning left towards Charing Cross station. Jay parks up around the corner from the hidden entrance. I spy Blizz, straddling Jay's bike and waiting for her next set of orders. Once we've stopped, she comes up to Jay's window and leans in.

'She's in there – she's put the place on emergency shutdown. It's being evacuated right now. Once you give her the order, she'll get to work,' she reports in her Eastern European tones.

'And how are things in Scotland?' Jay turns to Dozer, who is back on his phone.

'It's good, innit. They're all there. Even if they headed back now, it would be hours before they reached us. Even if Hayley Divine was going at top speed!' he replies.

'Then I guess we'd better get the two of you down there,' Jay says to me. Then it's a clap of hands and an unbuckling of seat belts before he opens the car door and yanks me out onto the street by my shoulder.

Blizz is over on the other side of the car, slapping Toby about the face with her cold hands to wake him up.

'Leave him alone,' I say, and she pauses to smirk at me, before continuing with her little game.

'What you do to him?' Blizz sighs at Dozer when it becomes apparent that she's not getting anywhere. 'He's not waking up.'

'Why don't we just finish him off now, boss? Save ourselves hassle, innit?' Dozer suggests, getting out of the car to try to wake Toby up himself.

'What would we do with a body?' Jay replies, and I shudder. What the hell are *we* going to do?

Toby answers the question for me. Somehow he's gone for Blizz. He's awake, and he's grappling with her, and when I bend down to get a better look I notice he's keeping his eyes closed to stop Dozer from putting him to sleep, so he doesn't know what he's hitting or where. He's just lashing out, all arms and legs as Blizz attempts to get close.

'Get away from me!' he yells, and I would use the opportunity to break free myself, but Jay's hand is gripping my arm, and my wrists are heavy and hurting from the ice.

Finally Blizz gets a lock on Toby, and he screams in pain as she freezes up his left arm. When she's done, she hurls him out of the car and Jay and Blizz force us both over to the entrance to the Strand. Dozer waits in the car; presumably he's the getaway driver.

The Strand looks the same as it did last time I was here. Grim railings and graffitied hoarding shields the site from passersby. The maroon ceramic tiles are the only clue that this was once the entrance to a bustling underground station. Jay pulls open the door with slightly too much force in his eagerness to get inside, and then starts punching codes into the security keypad before leading us down the spiral staircase I was forbidden access to before.

There's a red light flashing, dimming and lighting up our surroundings and, as we descend, we hear the loud wail of an emergency siren. Erica may have managed to get most of the people out of here, but surely there'll be some who'll stay, someone left here who can rescue us.

'Are you all right?' I mutter to Toby as we're both shoved and prodded like animals down the narrow staircase, Jay leading the way in front of me, and Blizz behind Toby at the back.

'My arm is so cold and heavy.' He shivers. 'What the hell are we doing? Where are we? What is this?'

'Calm down,' Jay snaps as we reach the bottom, stopping right in front of me.

It's as I suspected. Whatever fire alarm or emergency protocol Erica activated, there are still people down here, manning their posts and keeping the base secure. There's a guard or something, dressed all in black, standing with his back towards us just a little way ahead.

'Help!' I scream, getting his attention. I don't even have to think about yelling it.

The guard turns to face us but there's no time for him to act. Whippet fast, Blizz has come out from behind Toby and charged, a palm reaching out and striking the guard right in the solar plexus, freezing him statue-like in an instant.

'Don't do that!' Jay snaps at me, before catching himself and regaining his composure with a sly smile. 'Let's keep moving. And no funny business from either of you.'

I turn to look at Toby, whose face is ashen and terrified, his good arm supporting the numb one.

Sidestepping the frozen guard, Jay leads us down deserted corridors, some curved and reminiscent of their underground-station heritage, others stark and modern. All the time the siren is wailing and red emergency lights flash, making us look like red ghosts as we roam. Blizz and Jay are ahead of us now, both prepared for any more obstacles, while Toby and I linger behind, scared to do anything but follow.

When we get to an intersection, I take the risk. I grab Toby and dart down a side passage. Once we're out of sight, we run on, turning random corners and losing ourselves in the labyrinthine tunnels. I realise that Jay must know that we've gone, so I look for a place to hide, trying the doors on either side of us. Most are locked, no doubt because of the shutdown procedures Erica instigated, but finally, amazingly, a door opens. Toby shoves me into the darkness and then, with his good hand, he closes the door behind us.

Finally, in the dark, we can breathe. I feel for Toby, who is directly in front of me, but as I touch him he steps backwards with a jolt. My head fizzes with panic and I step back too, stumbling against some shelves that seem to be laden with boxes. We must be in some sort of supply cupboard.

'Sorry,' Toby stutters, his voice so quiet, still so scared.

'No, don't be sorry,' I say, even though I can't be entirely sure what it is that we're talking about. I desperately wish my hands were free right now, to push some hair back or rub my forehead with, but it's a little difficult, what with the cuffs. And boy, do they hurt. It's like shards of ice are permeating my skin, seeping through my veins.

'It's just, my arm,' Toby explains. 'I don't know what she's done. It's making me feel so cold.'

He stumbles further backwards, and even though I can't see him, I know that he's fallen to the floor.

'Toby?' I whisper.

'So cold,' he replies.

This can't be good. However much pain I'm feeling in my hands, Toby must be suffering worse. From what I can tell, Blizz has actually frozen his entire limb. What if his body can't cope with that? What if the cold sets in further and causes him permanent harm?

'Toby,' I say, 'I'm going to go and find Erica. She can warm you up and everything will be fine.'

'D-don't go,' Toby stutters, except it's not a stutter, but his teeth chattering from the cold.

'I have to. You're going to freeze to death or develop frostbite or something if I just stay here with you. I'm going to go and find Erica and stop all this madness, and then she'll save us both, OK?'

I don't wait for his reply. Somehow not being able to actually see him makes this decision a whole lot easier. If I can't see him, then maybe I won't feel so guilty about leaving him alone. I feel around for the door, and brace myself for the return of the red light and the siren sound. I lever my elbow down and the door opens. I work it slowly, aware that Jay could be waiting for me right outside. He's not. The wailing of the alarm hits me like thunder but thankfully the corridor is deserted in both directions. The red lights reflect off my manacles and they almost seem to glow.

I summon up all the ninja strength I had when I

escaped from my own house earlier this morning, and I run. I need to find Erica, and get her to burn these things off me and save Toby.

Is it too much to hope that there's an evacuation map somewhere? Apparently so. But there is a familiar green fire-escape sign above the doorway at one end of the corridor, so presumably if I go the opposite way I'll be heading into danger – and therefore towards Erica. I ponder the ludicrous nature of actually seeking danger instead of going away from it. Little me, who doesn't go near the school playground in case of wayward footballs, and who always starts her homework the night she gets it for fear of running out of time.

I run. I run down the corridor and through a set of fire doors that swing themselves shut again behind me. The place is a warren, but I charge through the abandoned network of corridors and tunnels because I know that Erica is here somewhere, and that I have to get to her before Jay catches up with me.

And then, breaking through one last set of double doors and into a giant cavern of a room, I find her.

20

I'm standing on some sort of gallery or balcony that looks down into a vast pit of a room. I can still hear the alarm but it sounds like it's outside; the noise is muted in here. This is the Vigil nerve centre. I know it is. One wall is taken up by a vast projection screen, inset with live feeds tracking Vigil activity all over the world, and a giant map showing all the global Vigil headquarters. There are rows and rows of deserted desks in the centre of the room, with partitioned offices and cubicles around the sides, and then, off in one corner, some sort of laboratory.

This room is what I've been dreaming of for the last couple of years. This is where it all happens, where decisions are made and lives are changed. Everything I've been searching for, all those Vigil secrets I've been dying to know, and now I'm here, *right here* in this room. It feels like that moment when you first enter a cathedral and can't quite take in the magnificence and scale of everything around you, and you can feel your heart beating in your chest.

'Erica!' I yell down. She's standing by a desk near the front, waiting for the phone to ring with Jay's command.

'Louise?' She's squinting as she peers up at me on the balcony; her mask has been laid aside nearby. 'What the hell are you doing here? You have to get out! Now!'

'No, Erica. Jay lied to you! He wants to trap me and Toby in here with you! You wouldn't have known...' My voice tails off as Erica flies up to meet me.

'Oh my God,' she sighs, placing her warm hands on either side of my face, holding me there as if checking that it's really me. 'Your hands!'

'Yeah, Blizz's handiwork. And she's done something to Toby too. He's hiding in a supply cupboard. We have to get to him so that you can warm him up. I think he might be seriously hurt.'

'And where is Jay now?'

'I don't know. We got away from him and hid, but I knew that I had to come out and find you. Erica – this all has to stop now. Jay is properly crazy! The Vigils need to get back here and arrest him or do something – you know, whatever superheroes do to super-villains!'

'First, your hands.' Erica propels herself over the railing so that she's standing with me on the balcony. She pauses, looking worried.

'What is it?' I ask, holding my hands out towards her. 'Please just defrost me already!'

'I don't want to hurt you,' she replies, obviously scared. 'How will I know when to stop the heat?'

'You'll be fine. I'll tell you when. Just please get them off me!'

She clasps her hot hand around my cuffs and almost instantly they melt away. Water drips and pools on the floor at my feet as slowly, carefully, Erica works at the ice. I suddenly regain feeling in my little finger and, looking down, I can see the colour of my hands is changing, no longer that sickly green-blue, but now blotchy red. Heat blooms through my bones and at first the feeling is akin to hugging a hot-water bottle on a cold night. It's comforting, and a huge relief. Except that as she continues, with the ice nearly gone and Erica still working at getting the heat through to my extremities, I start to feel pain. The sudden flow of blood to my fingers burns with the worst chilblains I have ever experienced. The pins and needles tickles like scurrying beetles across my palms, and as feeling comes back to my fingertips, they ache and cramp.

'OK, stop!' I warn, tugging my hands away from her and bringing them close to my chest for some comfort.

'How do they feel?' Erica asks.

'Fine,' I lie. 'Now let's go back to Toby!'

'Wait!' says Erica. 'I can use the computers here to get a message to the Vigils. We need to tell them what's going on. It won't take long, I promise!'

Launching herself over the railing, Erica glides down into the pit with the grace of a cat, all sleek energy and smooth lines. I, however, clang and rattle down the metal stairs. I couldn't feel more clumsy and cumbersome if I tried. When I'm down with her, Erica leads me through the maze of desks, stopping at one to input her password.

'You know how to use these computers?' I ask, nervous because Erica's never really shown much affinity for technology before.

'What do you think I've been doing these last few weeks? I even have my own personal Vigil email address!'

'Who could you possibly give that to?'

'It's more of an internal thing, to be honest. I can't even access it from my computer at home. But still – having it is pretty cool.'

Erica starts tapping away at the computer while I nurse my hands. The feeling is almost totally back now, but my wrists are still red and raw from the ice burn and my fingertips are bruised and sore. I take the opportunity to look around the room, padding carefully between the desks and glancing up at the massive screen displaying all the information. So much information. Some desks are piled high with files and paperwork, some are starkly empty. One has a vast chart with a supersuit design, complete with weapons schematics. I know that I shouldn't be here, that I shouldn't be snooping into all this top-secret knowledge, but the further away I wander from Erica, the bolder I feel in looking. I even sit down at one of the desks.

'Are you nearly done?' I call, thinking about Toby, hoping that he's OK and that I can remember the route back to him.

I swivel a bit in the chair and pretend to type at the keyboard (careful not to let my sore fingertips actually touch anything). My eyes flick up to the wall with the screen every now and again, as if I'm imagining that I really do work here. It would be so amazing if I did, for even the tiniest bit of this to be mine.

Then I shiver. I shrug it off at first, because obviously my body temperature is still adjusting due to my hands, but it happens again. The air in here is definitely colder, and by now I know what that means.

I make a split-second decision not to call out to Erica. She hasn't sensed that Blizz is close, but I figure that I'm the most vulnerable here and I need to hide. I slink down in the chair and under the desk, hoping that Blizz hasn't seen me yet. Once again the adrenaline surges, making me itchy and jumpy, and as I wait I notice my breath clouding out in front of me.

'Erica!' It's Jay. He must be with Blizz. I didn't get a chance to look up to the balcony and I can't see anything from my hiding place, but I can hear the staircase giving its metallic rattle as they descend.

I wish I could see where Erica is, because I don't hear her answer. But now, from my position curled on the floor,

I can see Blizz. She glides by the desk next to me, and as her fingers dance over the surface, it crusts over with ice crystals, beautiful like diamonds. The air around her shimmers with frosted dust. I curl myself up into the tightest ball I can manage, trying to keep myself warm.

'It's over, Jay,' I can hear Erica call. 'I've sent out an alert and told the Vigils everything. They're heading back here. You're in big trouble.'

'Oooh, I'm scared,' Jay replies, half laughing. Voices carry in this cavernous space, and his laugh echoes.

'Keep away from me,' Erica warns, but I can hear the wobble in her voice. I want to tell her that it's going to be fine, that she can take both Blizz and Jay down if she really wants to, and that she shouldn't be scared. 'I mean it. Stay back!'

There's a rumble behind me, and the desk shakes with pressure. It's heat. Erica, out of my sight, is fighting back. I'm desperate to get out of my hiding place and see what's going on, but the thought of Jay catching me and doing something terrible to distract Erica forces me to hold on and stay hidden. I nearly bite right through my lip with the tension.

And then Jay's right there. He's still wearing his stupid trench coat, and his boots are only inches from my face. All he has to do is look down and I'll be caught. I can't let that happen. He's stopped right next to me and is spouting off to Erica about his vision or purpose or something. I haven't got time to listen to another one of his maniacal speeches. As I shove my sore hands into my pockets for warmth, I find the USB cable I stowed in there earlier. If this was a cartoon, a bright light bulb would have popped up over my head right now.

In one swift and silent move, I reach out and wrap the cable around one of Jay's legs. Before he's even registered that something's amiss, I tug with all of my strength and Jay topples, crashing to the floor and flat on his face. *Yes!* And then, in my own version of a crazy awesome ninja move, I kick out the wheelie desk chair – with enough force that it ploughs straight into him. There's an audible *oof* of pain.

I crawl out from under the desk, scampering as quickly as I can to get away from Jay, aware that as thrillingly awesome as my ninja moves are, they're hardly going to take him out of action for very long.

I look over to Erica. It's like watching a film. I can't believe that this is anything other than some incredible, computer-generated effect. Blizz is sending a charge of frozen air out from her hands towards Erica, and in retaliation Erica's hands have manifested the largest flames I've ever seen her produce. It's as if she's got blowtorches for fingers and she's trying to push forward, forcing Blizz back. It's an intimidating sight, watching someone try to destroy your best friend, but I have faith in Erica and I know that she'll win.

Except I can see the pain in her face, and the exhaustion this whole thing is causing. In comparison, Blizz looks comfortable, like she's finding this easy, a wicked smile creeping across her face as Erica strains to throw all she can muster at her. In response, Blizz starts pushing forward, the cold air whipping about her in white flurries. Erica's whole body is glowing with effort, her hair a wild halo behind her as every part of her distorts through the haze of heat. It's fire versus ice, and where their powers meet there is a swirling vortex of red-gold and blue.

I've forgotten about Jay. He's up again, and lumbering towards me, his hands tensed into claws and dripping something – it's ink. That dark revolting stuff is seeping from his pores, and as he stumbles against desks he leaves behind handprints like demonic ink blots. I've got no superpowers to help me. I'm trapped, and the only way out that I know of is back up those stairs to the gallery.

I look around me for something I can use. The desk next to me is cluttered with files and folders, but there's also a mug of tea just sitting there, probably left to get cold when Erica evacuated the place. I pick it up, and in what I already realise is a rather futile move to gain some time, I chuck the contents at Jay. Unfortunately he is not a storybook witch and he does not fizzle to his demise. He just leers at me and wipes the cold tea from his brow.

'Someone's got themselves caught up in a game they can't handle,' he says, edging closer.

I force myself to break my gaze with him so that I can see what's going on across the room. Erica and Blizz are still fighting, but it looks more like dancing, one creeping forward as the other retreats. But it's Erica who is dominating, taking the lead. This gives me confidence.

'Just give up, Jay! You're bonkers, you know that? Sure, you have some good ideas, but you don't get what you want by blowing stuff up! That just makes people angry, and scared. It doesn't make them listen!' I yell.

I look around me again, wondering if it's even in me to do something violent enough to put Jay out of action. And then I remember Toby, probably dying of hypothermia in a dark cupboard in a corridor I can't even remember how to get back to. If he was here instead of me, he'd be fighting – maybe flailing – but definitely *trying* to win. I can't give up. I guess this is what the expression 'do or die' means.

My eyes fall on a staple gun. I'm gripping the handle before I can even think this through, and then surging forward with one arm outstretched, ready to pull at the trigger when I get close enough.

Jay's trying to grapple at me with his disgustingly slimy hands, and I can feel them sliding around over my top, but all that ink means that he's not able to grip. I reach under and around him and fire the staple gun, right into his neck, under the jaw. And then again, striking him on the forehead and behind the ear. I nearly get the gun tangled up in his ridiculous hair, but I shuffle and pull free with just enough time to get him right on the cheek. Each click of the gun gives a satisfying release until finally he has to stagger back, feeling himself for injury with hands that leave smears of dark blue all over his face.

'What the hell?' he asks, before one of Erica's heat pulses finds him and he falls forward, flat onto his face for a second time, only now he doesn't get back up.

I turn back to Erica. By taking one of her hands away to pummel Jay, she's given Blizz some leeway. This isn't good. Now it's Erica taking steps backwards, and Blizz driving forward with all that cold shooting out from her.

Heading to another desk, I see that it's frustratingly sparse and tidy, and at first I fear that there'll be nothing there to help me, but then I see a stationery organiser. And in there is an ordinary rubber eraser. I reach around the desk to pick it up, along with a plastic ruler. Blizz is standing about five metres away and is far too focused on Erica to notice anything in her peripheral vision, but Erica spots what I'm up to – I'm almost directly in her line of sight.

I place the rubber at the end of the ruler and prepare to flick. I can feel my heart hammering in my chest and I bite at my lip in concentration while I pull the ruler back and line it up with Blizz. Erica, realising what I'm about to do, appears to have gathered a little more strength. Her eyes are focused and intense, her arms held strong in front of her against the barrage of ice. I have to get this right.

I let go. The rubber seems to fly in slow motion through the air in a perfect arc across the vast room. It smacks directly on Blizz's temple. For just a tiny moment, barely even a second, she pauses to turn and see where it came from. That's all Erica needs. She charges forward with a burst of energy, and Blizz just can't recover quickly enough. She staggers backwards, her control slipping, until finally Erica is standing over her, pummelling her with heat until she relents and collapses on the floor.

'Erica!' I call out, relieved and proud, but she doesn't even glance up. The air sparks with energy as she looms over Blizz, who's now cowering in fear. Erica's wearing the same expression that she had that time by the tree.

'Erica!' I call again. 'You can stop now!'

She pauses. The heat has stopped but she's still standing there, stunned and panting, obviously ready for another round. By the time I get over to them she's managed to relax her fists but I have to actually touch her shoulder – just briefly before I recoil from the heat – to get her to look at me. As soon as she does I realise that she's back, and she's not going to cause any unnecessary harm. Blizz lies on the floor, defeated and exhausted.

'Are you all right?' I ask Erica.

'Yeah, I'm fine,' she pants. 'What about you?'

'I'm good,' I say.

We stare at each other for a moment, both of us smiling and close to tears, before finally she lunges towards me and clasps me close. Despite the burning heat, I hug her right back.

21

Having a 'situation debrief' isn't nearly as exciting as I thought it was going to be. After a day of frenzied running about, escaping from Jay's evil clutches, I ought to be relieved. Only thing is, it feels more like an interrogation.

The man opposite me reminds me of my deputy head, Mr Stanley. They both have the same kind of face, pinched in at the eyes and with barely any top lip. The difference is that this guy seems devoid of any sense of humour. He watches me closely, looking for signs of – what exactly? That I might be lying? That I might be one of the bad guys? I'm annoyed that he doesn't seem to trust me. I use every bit of my teacher's pet charm, but he sits rigid and unsmiling. Maybe before all this happened I would be scared of him, but right now I'm tired and impatient, and just want to get back outside to Erica.

'And what can you tell us about Copyboy's accomplices?' he asks, slowly like I might not understand him.

'Blizz and Dozer? We never really got the chance to chat,' I reply.

'You said Dozer was on the phone a lot?'

'Yes...'

'Who was he talking to?'

'I have absolutely no idea. Have you asked *him*?'

'We think he was talking with Copyboy's accomplices in Scotland, the ones who sabotaged the power plant. Did you hear anything that might corroborate this?'

'Nope. Nothing. I didn't really get a chance to snoop on his conversation. I was really too preoccupied with, you know, being held hostage and very nearly murdered?'

The nameless man, a non-superpowered agent of the Vigil organisation, sneers a little when he looks up at me. I think I'm meant to be intimidated. I'm not.

'We'd appreciate your cooperation in this matter, Ms Kirby,' he says, looking back down at his notes.

'I've told you the whole story,' I insist. 'And I've had a really long day. Plus we've been sitting here for over an hour now. Please can you just tell me everything's going to be fine? You've got them all, right?'

He places his pen down on his jotter pad and seems to relax slightly. I guess it's been a long day for him too.

'All three are in custody, and we have agents closing in on further accomplices. You'll be fine, Ms Kirby. We can give you a number to call if you feel that your safety or security are compromised, but we don't anticipate any repercussions from this incident. Copyboy – Jay – was the primary instigator, and trust me, he's going to be locked up for a very long time.'

When I'm let go and taken back into the main room – or Mission Room as apparently it's meant to be called – I feel dizzy. Being underground and under artificial lighting does strange things to your senses, especially when you're already tired and mentally wiped out. It's not like a complete catastrophic zone of destruction in here, but Erica and Blizz's fight hardly left things clean and tidy. There are people all around us checking the computers and moving bits and pieces of wreckage out of the way, some of it singed black, some frozen solid.

'Toby!' I practically race down the staircase from the gallery when I see him standing there, his arm appearing to be back at normal body temperature. 'I was so worried!'

He's really not prepared for me flinging my arms around him. It's the awkward cough of a nearby Vigil agent that makes us finally back away from one another, and now I have no idea where to stand or what to do. Neither does Toby. He shoves his hands in his pockets and does that awkward bounce-on-his-heels thing that I've seen him do before.

'How are you feeling?' I ask.

'Surprisingly good! Erica warmed everything back up. Arm still stings a little, but otherwise everything seems fine. No need to cut any of my fingers off from frostbite quite yet.' He sounds nervous. I am nervous.

'I kind of feel like I was a bit of a coward back there,' he admits.

'Why would you think that?'

'Oh, I don't know. That pretending to be asleep thing, so that I could fight back, was hardly effective, and you know, completely wimping out on you in that cupboard. Not exactly a move to be proud of.'

'Tobes, you were injured. There was nothing you could do. Besides, everything has worked out just fine. I honestly don't know how I would have coped without you today. It's been epic.'

'I don't know. This wasn't exactly what I imagined visiting Vigil HQ would be like.'

The place is now swarming with Vigil agents. They made their grand entrance soon after Erica and I finished our little battle scene and haven't left us alone since. They're busy worker bees all in black, scurrying around and checking computers for any signs of corruption or infiltration. The actual superhero guys are still up in Scotland, but they're heading home, having made sure that the nuclear power plant is completely safe. I'm secretly hoping that they make it back before we have to go home, but maybe it isn't the best time to be meeting Quantum and the gang. For starters, I must look like a frazzled mess, and my wrist and hands, although recovered (I've already been checked by a Vigil doctor), still feel a little weird. What I want more than anything is to be at home in a nice hot bubble bath. Definitely not the ideal frame of mind to be in when meeting one of the most powerful people on the planet.

'Are you sure you're OK?' I ask Toby. He's still shuffling a bit on his feet and looking pensive.

'It's just...'

'What?'

'You know how I was so great and calm earlier, and how well I was handling everything back at Jay's place?'

'Yeah?'

'Well, can I freak out now? Like, really actually properly freak out?'

'It depends on what that entails...' I say nervously, looking around the vast chamber at all the very important people doing their very important jobs and hoping that he doesn't make a spectacle of himself.

'WHAT THE HELL, LOUISE?!' Apparently Toby doesn't do freak-outs by half.

'Calm down...' I insist.

'CALM DOWN? WE'RE STANDING IN A VIGIL MISSION ROOM AND YOU'RE TELLING ME TO CALM DOWN?' His lanky arms flail in all directions, and he paces around in a tiny circle.

'Toby...' I edge closer to him, blushing with embarrassment, but hoping that somehow he might be able to focus a bit if I can just manage to look him in the eyes.

'WE WERE KIDNAPPED AND I HIT SOME GUY WITH A VASE AND HE PUT ME TO SLEEP AND THEN WE WERE KIDNAPPED AGAIN AND MY ARM GOT FROZEN SOLID AND YOU LEFT ME IN A CUPBOARD.' He pauses, staring at the floor for a moment. 'You have no idea how scared I was when you went away.'

'Toby.' I'm right up close to him, looking up because he's so annoyingly tall, and somehow my hands have found his, and what's really strange is that this doesn't feel awkward at all. There have been so many times when I've imagined this, just the simple thing of holding his hand, and now here we are, and I'm wondering why it was ever such a big deal.

Maybe it's the tiredness, or maybe my adventure today has affected me more than I'd realised, but I'm feeling brave and reckless. For the first time in a heck of a long time, I'm not just Erica's sidekick, a secondary character in her epic story. Erica has her world, and I'll always be a part of it somehow, but I have my world too, and maybe it's time that I started living in it. I look up again at Toby, with his grey eyes and his crazy hair that flies up at impossible angles, and suddenly I don't care about consequences. All that matters is that I feel it, and even if what happens next doesn't go the way I want, at least it was something that I made happen all by myself.

I reach up on tiptoes and kiss him.

It's the tiniest moment, and he barely responds

because he's caught off-guard, but I've done it. I've wanted to do it for longer than I'd dare to admit. Whatever happens next, at least I've done it.

'What was that for?' Toby asks, his voice now calm and soft, his lips, the ones that I just touched with mine, tipping into a gentle smile.

'Well, it was partly to get you to shut up, and partly just because I wanted to.'

'You just wanted to? Just like that? For absolutely no reason whatsoever? Because I'll be honest with you, I'm not entirely feeling at my most attractive right now, and I would have much preferred you wanting to when I was in a much more manly and dignified situation, you know?'

'Shut up, Toby!' And I reach up to kiss him again, this time longer and more definite, just in case there was any question about what happened before.

'Ugh, get a room, you guys!' It's Erica, slinking up on us from wherever she's been for the last hour or so, probably being debriefed by agents like I was.

'Erica!' I cry, letting Toby go so that I can hug her. 'How are you?'

'I'll be fine. I'm worn out, but the doc has checked me over and I've had my first debrief, and it looks like everything is going to be fine. And I mean, actually, properly fine now. Not the *Oh, I'm sure everything will turn out OK, probably* kind of fine.'

'I'm glad to hear it,' I say.

'Still, I think I might have pissed off quite a few people here.'

'What do you mean?' Toby asks.

'Well, being the new kid is hard enough, but when it also turns out that I seem to be accompanied by Trouble with a capital T, I'm not exactly making loads of friends.'

'But it wasn't your fault about Jay,' I insist. 'He fooled everyone, not just you. This is not your fault, and don't let anyone tell you otherwise.'

'See.' Erica turns to Toby. 'This is why she's such a good friend.' Turning back to me: 'You may not realise it, but I swear that Sensible Voice of yours is one hell of a superpower.'

'It'll take some time to make new friends here, but it'll all work out.' I smile. 'So what happens now?'

'I think I have to stay here for a bit, but you two can go. Let me check with someone.'

Erica scurries away, just about managing to dodge the two agents carrying away a charred slab of desk. I see her apologise awkwardly to them, and realise that despite the bravado, inside she must be disappointed about the way things turned out.

A figure up on the gallery catches my eye. She holds onto the railing, peering around the pit in wonder, but her face is blotchy, like she's been crying.

'It's Liza,' I mumble.

'Who?' Toby asks, following my gaze.

'Erica's mum is here. She was so worried about Erica going missing that I guess the Vigils decided to bring her in.'

'Did she know?'

'About the superpowers? I'm not entirely sure that she knows even now.'

We watch as Liza is escorted down the stairs and into the pit. She sees me and her face freezes. Ignoring the agents on either side of her, she marches right up to me, and I flinch because I'm so certain that she's going to hurt me.

'Why didn't you tell me about this?' Her eyes are livid with anger. For the first time it occurs to me that there might be a genetic source for Erica's power.

'I couldn't,' I reply.

'You should have told me. My own daughter! Somebody should have told me! Why should I find out like this? I've been frantic this past week! Going out of my mind!'

'She should have told you, but we didn't know how. It was too difficult. We didn't tell anybody.'

'Tell me, Louise, does she hate me that much? Does she really think that I wouldn't still love her, or care? She's my daughter. We may not have the most typical of relationships, but she's still my daughter, and she should have told me about this.'

'Mum.' Erica's standing just a little way away, but doesn't look as if she wants to come any closer.

'Erica!' Liza says, throwing her hands down in futility. It's the first time she's seen her daughter in her costume, the first time she's been able to see her for who she really is.

'Please don't shout at my friends,' Erica says, her voice soft and scared.

'Why couldn't you tell me about this?' Liza pleads. She takes a step closer, but it's not close enough.

'Seriously, how was I meant to tell you, Mum? Every time we talk we end up fighting. I could never know how you were going to react.'

'You should have told me,' Liza repeats, her words broken up by sobs.

Toby comes to stand behind me and places a hand on my shoulder.

'I didn't know they were bringing you in,' Erica says. 'I mean, I knew that you were going to have to come in eventually, but I didn't know that it was going to be now. What have they told you?'

'They told me you have powers. Like those people on the telly.'

'That's right.'

'They said that you were in danger.'

'I was, but it's all fine now. Louise saved me.'

'Is that right?' Liza turns to look at me, but I look away, embarrassed.

'Maybe we should go somewhere quiet and talk about this,' Erica suggests. Liza nods in agreement, and after

Erica signals to a nearby agent, they're both led away to one of the debrief rooms.

'Are they going be all right?' Toby asks me.

'I hope so,' I reply.

It's time to leave, and Toby and I are accompanied back up the staircase to the gallery, and then through the maze of corridors and to a lift that will take us back up to street level. One of them presses the button to call the lift. The agents don't talk to us. They're probably really annoyed at all the hassle we've caused.

The lift arrives, and Toby is the one who gasps when the doors open, because I'm too busy staring down at my feet. But when I finally do look up I have one of those moments where I wonder if my brain is able to tell the difference between reality and fantasy any more. Because this can't possibly be real. For starters, he's huge. He's a megalith of a human being, all height and breadth and arms and torso. And the mask is off. Good God, the mask is off.

'Good evening, sir,' one of the agents says as Quantum steps out of the lift. 'We weren't expecting you until much later.'

'I took the jet. Because apparently you kids can't look after the place properly when Daddy's gone. Who are these two?'

Quantum has short, dirty-blond hair. Nobody else knows that — nobody outside of this base anyway.

251

Because how would they know, when he goes around saving the world in a mask all the time? He has dirty-blond hair that's cut military short, but with enough height at the front to make a nice tuft above his forehead. He has eyebrows. I can't believe this, but Quantum actually has eyebrows. Not that I didn't think he would have eyebrows, because he is a person after all, but in all the footage and all the photos I've researched over the last few years, how could I ever have known for sure? He has eyebrows, and cheeks, and the tiniest hint of a hook in his hawk-like nose. It's Quantum. Right here. Right now. And he's asking who I am.

'These are the kids who saved the day,' the agent replies. And there I was thinking that they hated us!

'What are your names?' He looks to Toby first, but Toby can't speak. Toby looks like he's been totally frozen solid all over again.

'I'm Louise, and this is Toby. We're Erica's friends,' I just about manage to gurgle out.

'Well, it's very nice to meet you, Louise and Toby. And thanks for saving the day. Usually that's our job, but it's nice to know that you've got our backs.' He runs his fingers through his hair, mussing it up. He looks normal, and kind, and OH MY GOD, HE KNOWS MY NAME.

He starts to move away, and the agents either side of us move around him to get into the lift. Toby, jaw still locked in awe, shuffles in after them, keeping his gaze fixed on Quantum. The doors are just about to close, and he's walking away, and who knows what's got into me, but I can't let him just leave.

'Mr Quantum!' I call out, jamming the lift doors back open with my hand.

He turns.

'I don't suppose there's any chance I could get some work experience here, could I?'

22

I'm lying on my bed, and there's a book propped open on my chest that I'm meant to be reading for school on Monday, except that it's impossible to read when there's a boy sitting cross-legged on the floor next to you, biting his lip while he doodles in his sketchpad. I keep stopping mid-sentence.

'Just tell me what you're drawing,' I moan.

'Nope, can't,' Toby replies. 'It's a surprise.'

The last week has been hard. The Vigil people wanted me to spend it at home – they said that I should recuperate from my adventure, but I think they just wanted to make sure any potential media attention would die down by the time I went back to school. There was a fear that the story would leak and my name would get out, and the term 'lying low' got bandied about, but I decided that I couldn't take any time off school. Not with exams looming. They weren't as impressed with my steely resolve as I thought they would be.

School was strange, because of course nobody knew

what had happened, yet I felt totally different. I felt taller, if that makes any sense. Taller and somehow more substantial. Looking people in the eye doesn't feel nearly so scary any more. Is this what confidence is? It's like having a secret identity of my own: Louise Kirby, by day a mild-mannered schoolgirl, by night a total badass.

As it turned out, there weren't any media problems to manage. We emerged above ground that Saturday to find the world continuing just as it had before. The sun had set and the streetlights had come on, and people walked past us, oblivious to what had gone on just under their feet. Toby and I were put in a taxi home together, but we were too tired to talk. He did surprise me though, about halfway through the journey, when he reached out and took my hand as it lay on the central armrest. I hardly even noticed it at first, but when I did, I managed to give his hand a gentle squeeze, as if to say, in my own quiet way, that things were going to be fine.

'OK, I'm done!' Toby exclaims at last, setting down his pens and holding his sketchbook out.

He's drawn a caricature of me wearing a mask and a cape, soaring across the white expanse of the page. I think that maybe he's made my cheeks a little too hamster-like, but it's cute. It's so very cute.

'So, I'm a superhero now, am I?' I tease, not able to keep the smile from my face. 'What's my power, then?'

'Generally just being awesome,' Toby says, mirroring my grin.

Toby's had a lot to deal with at home over the past week. After cultivating his perfect 'good teen' image with his parents, the front room covered in tiny shards of frosted glass was a little hard to explain. He also had to sign loads of forms and have lengthy interviews about how he got caught up in everything.

We're disturbed by a rap at the window, and we turn to see a masked face there, and a little hand waving and impatient. Toby jumps up to let Erica in.

'I hope I'm not interrupting anything?' she says with a smirk, before coming over to give me a hug. 'So, how's it going, Tobes?'

It turns out that one week isn't really enough time for Toby to adjust to Erica – the Erica he's seen around school for years – being a superhero. Plus there's all the awkward fanboy stuff to contend with whenever he encounters her in full costume. Despite everything we've been through, especially all the frozen-melty stuff, he still reacts to her as if she's this glittering, unapproachable celebrity who generously deigns to speak with him. Of course Erica milks it for all she can.

'Yeah, I'm fine,' Toby mumbles. 'I should probably get going though?'

'You're not going to stay and girl talk?' Erica pulls her mask up and off her face.

'I'd better not. There's this essay I've got . . . and it's due in . . .'

'See you later, Tobes?' I ask, and at my voice he instantly relaxes.

'Yeah, see you later!' He scuttles out of my room, nearly banging his head on the door frame as he goes.

'He is so ridiculously cute!' Erica comments after him, before sliding down beside me on my bed.

'So, how is everything?' I ask.

'It's all good. They haven't charged me for any of the damage in the Mission Room, if that's what you mean. But forget about that – tell me about you! How's Toby?'

'It's nice. He's nice,' is all I can admit without blushing.

'Look at you, all loved up. I knew it would happen with him. I knew it!'

As easy as it would be to tell her everything about Toby, I hope she doesn't mind that I want to keep it to myself right now. It's just that it's so new, and I think I might deserve some secrets of my own for the first time.

'What about you? Are you coming back to school any time soon?' Unlike me, Erica has chosen to take all the time off that she's allowed. Partly so that she can focus on her training, but also so she can start spending some quality time with her mum.

'So about that,' she starts, and the pause that follows makes me hold my breath. 'It's just that I feel like I have so much work to do, you know? All that power, and I'm so scared of losing control. And it's not as if I can leave it for later. I have to start now, if I'm going to have the future I want. But with everything that's happened, it's been suggested that I think about moving somewhere else until I'm ready for the big league.'

'So what does that mean? Are you going to the Paris team?' I could manage Paris. A few hours on the train would mean loads of fun days out.

'No.' She pauses again, and doesn't look me in the eyes. 'They want me to go to New York, to be part of the team over there.'

'You said no, right? Because of your age and your mum and everything else? You can't go to New York!'

'I can. I'm going over there to finish my education, and to train with Solar and the rest of the East Coast team. It's all been arranged. That's what I've come over to tell you.'

I'm waiting for that feeling to overcome me, the bitter taste of rage and hurt. But it doesn't arrive. Instead what I feel is an unexpected stillness. I wonder if I'm in shock and whether a reaction will come later, but right now there's just a vaguely pleasant quietness that keeps me calm. Yes, the thought of Erica being an ocean away isn't great, but I can also see her doing a huge amount of good out there.

'OK, then.' My lips are numb as I say the words, as if I can't quite believe that I'm saying them.

'OK?'

'Yeah. I can see you really liking New York. I think you'd be perfect out there.'

'For some reason I thought you'd be angry with me or something. And anyway, I'll be home to visit loads, and there's always the internet. I can see us chatting more than we do now!'

'I would have thought I'd be angry too,' I admit, 'but I really think this is right for you. What does your mum say?'

'She's excited. She's been looking for a way to leave for ages and make a new start. I think this will be good for her too, for both of us. No more secrets. And I've still got so much to learn. It'll be nice to start over with people who don't already know me and what I've done.'

'What's going to happen to Jay?' I ask.

'The Vigils have their own ways of dealing with people like him. Let's just say he won't be causing any trouble for the foreseeable future.' She pauses. 'You know what I've been thinking, though?'

'What?'

'That Jay was right about a lot of things. So much about how the Vigils work nowadays has to do with PR and branding and monetising. And even though he was clearly completely mad, he wasn't completely wrong.'

'Here's what I think,' I start. 'I think that you need to remember who you are, and your own heroes. Think of the Amazing Clara and everything she did. If you don't like how things are working, you can change things. You can be that person who changes things for the better, but from the inside out. Be the superhero you always wanted to be, and the others will follow. You can be – the Amazing Vega!'

She reaches over and hugs me, a tight squeeze that makes my eyes bulge. I don't think she even realises how strong she is now.

'I love you, you know that?' she whispers into my ear.

'I love you too. We're family, right?'

'Definitely!' When she releases me she turns away quickly, but not before I catch the faint sizzle of a tear evaporating from her hot cheek. 'So, have you got too much homework to do, or can we watch a film or some-thing? Also, can I borrow some clothes? Because it is absolutely impossible to relax in this costume!'

I stick a film on my laptop, but to be honest we hardly watch it. We're too busy chatting about everything we can think of. It reminds me of before, when she'd come over and tell me about her schoolfriends, about who fancied who, who was failing history and who had stolen a bottle of vodka from their parents. But now, instead of the likes of Annabel or Heather, it's Hayley Divine she's gushing about. Who'd have thought that the crazy intricacies and social politics of a legion of superheroes would be so similar to life in the playground?

'I should probably get going,' she says as the credits start to roll.

'You could stay here for a bit longer if you like.'

'No, I should go. But I miss this, you know? I miss just being able to come round here and tell you anything. I miss how things were.'

'Things were always going to change,' I say. 'Even if you were completely normal, we'd be doing different things at college, and then university. We're not kids any more.'

'I guess this is growing up, right?'

'A part of it maybe.'

I help her back into her costume and then open the window.

'Best friends for ever?' she asks, and she really means it, like her life might depend on the answer.

'Best friends for ever,' I confirm.

'You're awesome, you know that?' she whispers. Then she pushes herself onto my window ledge, finding her balance as she prepares to fly away. I think before everything happened I would have shrugged off a statement like that, but right now I kind of believe her. I do feel a little bit awesome, just being me.

I recognise a hesitation in her, an unwillingness to go, and that's all I need to realise that whatever happens in the future, we'll always be there for each other. She turns, and there's that familiar flash of mischievous grin, before she's off into the clouds and on to whatever adventure comes next.

Acknowledgements

Firstly to my parents, Nigel and Elaine, and my brother James: your love and support has meant everything to me. I'm lucky to have such a large family, every single one of whom has offered nothing but kindness and encouragement along this whole journey. Thank you.

Bryony Woods, my agent, you spotted something in me all that time ago, and I am forever grateful that you did. I couldn't have survived this process without you! To Charlie Sheppard and Chloe Sackur and all the team at Andersen Press, thank you for believing in Louise and Erica, and for helping me bring them to life.

To all my colleagues at Waterstones, especially the incredible people I've worked with at Piccadilly, thank you so much. Nicky, Leah, Mary, Peter, Roger, Eva, Pete, Amber and Cam especially – look! I put your names in the back of my book! My other bookselling chums, Teresa, Lisa and Jenn, you just don't know what your friendship has meant to me over the last few years.

Huge thank yous must go to my teachers on the

Birkbeck Creative Writing MA: Toby Litt, Julia Bell and Michael Rosen. And to those misfits I met in Toby's class (we imaginatively named ourselves Toby's People), none of you had the guts to name one of your children after Toby, but I did! But seriously, guys, thank you.

To the manager and all the staff at Edgware Starbucks, thank you for letting me write my novel (and rewrite it, and rewrite it again) in your fine establishment. I'm also lucky to have found a real community of friends here, long live the Edgware Skcubrats!

I've had four wonderful guides through the world of comic books: Dan, Jim, Adrian and Eli. You guys have been terrific enablers, thank you for welcoming me into your world with open arms and enthusiasm.

To my closest friends: Lisa, Michelle, Vic, Alice, Ben and Laura-Jane. Whether you live near or far or overseas, this is a book about friendship, and it's you who have taught me all about it. I love you guys for ever.

There have been a vast quantity of writers I have met along this journey – you know who you are – and every single one of you has been an inspiration.

A special thanks must go to The Arts Council, which has provided me with the means over the last year to bring this book to fruition.

And finally, to Cameron Krokatsis, the one person who I wish could read this, but never will.